Lisa stared out the window at the full moon and dreamed of Rick. What was he doing right this minute? Was he sitting by his own window, staring at the same moon and dreaming of her? If only it were true! Then Lisa closed her eyes and sent Rick a message. "Call me. Love me. Love me."

For a moment, the feeling was so strong she almost expected the phone to ring. She sat curled in her chair, eyes closed, and waited for a long time. Even when she finally went to bed, she held on to the dream.

Maybe, just maybe, Rick received her message. Maybe, in time, he would act on it.

Dear Reader,

At Silhouette we publish books with you in mind. We're pleased to announce the creation of Silhouette First Love, a new line of contemporary romances written by the finest young-adult writers as well as outstanding new authors in this field.

Silhouette First Love captures many of the same elements enjoyed by Silhouette Romance readers—love stories, happy endings and the same attention to detail and description. But First Love features young heroines and heroes in contemporary and recognizable situations.

You play an important part in our future plans for First Love. We welcome any suggestions or comments on our books and I invite you to write to us at the address below.

Karen Solem
Editor-in-Chief
Silhouette Books
P.O. Box 769
New York, N.Y. 10019

FLOWERS
FOR LISA
Veronica Ladd

First Love from Silhouette
Published by Silhouette Books New York
America's Publisher of Contemporary Romance

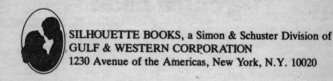 SILHOUETTE BOOKS, a Simon & Schuster Division of
GULF & WESTERN CORPORATION
1230 Avenue of the Americas, New York, N.Y. 10020

Copyright © 1981 by Veronica Ladd

Distributed by Pocket Books

ISBN: 0-671-53305-3

First Silhouette Books printing October, 1981

10 9 8 7 6 5 4 3 2 1

America's Publisher of Contemporary Romance

Printed in the U.S.A.

For L. L.
Romantic Hero,
Leading Man
in My Private Movie

1

Lisa Kelly looked out the window at the grumpy gray sky. How could anyone concentrate on spring flowers in miserable weather like this? She sighed and turned back to the drawing of daffodils and tulips she was working on, adding a spot of blue to the edge of the leaves. When she was finished, she looked critically at her work and shook her head. The assignment would be another B-minus disaster.

Reluctantly, she carried her drawing to Ms. Martino. Though she knew the art teacher would always find something to say that was encouraging, she also knew that this work was another failure. Why did I ever sign up for art? Lisa asked herself. Then she smiled grimly. She'd signed up for art because Rick Brewster would be in the class. At least she could tell herself that truth.

Lisa waited patiently beside Ms. Martino's desk, listening to her tell another student how to balance the design on his paper. "Think of each flower as weighing as much as lead. Would your paper tip to the right or the left?" Ms. Martino asked.

As the boy admitted his paper tilted to the right, Ms. Martino bobbed her head up and down enthusiastically. "That's right. Now go fix it." Then she turned to Lisa and asked, "Now, my Irish beauty, what have you to show me?"

Lisa blushed as she did each time the art teacher called her a beauty. At first Lisa had thought she was making fun of her because she was too tall and too thin, but she'd soon discovered that Ms. Martino never made fun of people. No, Ms. Martino must think she was nice-looking. Lisa pushed aside the depressing thought that her art teacher was the only one. No one else ever called her pretty.

Brushing back the long black bangs that fell into her eyes with one hand, she held out her drawing of spring flowers to Ms. Martino with the other hand. "This assignment is late," she said. "I had a hard time with it."

But Ms. Martino was not the sort of teacher who bothered with whether or not an assignment was late; she looked at each work with an interested eye. Now she held Lisa's drawing up, turning it slowly from side to side to catch the light. Lisa hung her head in despair. She knew it wasn't great, but she had hoped that Ms. Martino would find something good to say about it. She usually did praise at least one thing in a work, but now she was very silent.

Lisa opened her mouth to make excuses, hating herself for her need to apologize, but before she could begin, Ms. Martino called out, "Class, drop whatever you're doing and come here!"

Oh, no! Lisa thought. She was going to use her work to show the whole class something. Probably something awful, like how not to draw a tulip. Lisa felt her face burning as everyone in the art class moved closer to the teacher's desk. Out of the corner of her eye, Lisa could see Rick Brewster moving toward her. Her heart began to beat faster as she realized that Rick was going to stand next to her. No matter how humiliating the lesson turned out to be, she was going to be close to Rick. That was worth something!

"Now, this is a perfect design," Ms. Martino said to the group. Lisa felt a rush of relief run through her body. No matter what other grim things Ms. Martino might find to say, at least she'd said the design was perfect.

Ms. Martino traced a long, thin finger along the stem of the tallest flower up to the blossom at the top of the page. "Notice the simple, clean sweep of the stems. The plain treatment of the flower petals. Most important, see the way Lisa has left the blank white space on the left. She lets the white space balance the flowers, and it works. Look carefully; what else do you see?" She held the drawing toward the class, waiting expectantly.

Lisa, who was still looking at her feet, heard a deep, warm voice beside her say, "The little strip of blue is balancing the tips of yellow. It's just right."

"Exactly!" Ms. Martino smiled at Rick and said, "You picked up on the most subtle part of the design." Then she handed the drawing back to Lisa and said, "Cut a mat for it and we'll put it on the hall display board."

"I'm a first-year student," Lisa reminded her. "I don't know how to cut mats yet."

"Rick, cut the mat for Lisa, will you?" Ms. Martino asked.

Rick smiled at Lisa and said, "Sure. Come on over here."

The class went back to work and Lisa followed Rick Brewster over to the table where he worked each day. As she walked behind him she hoped he wouldn't be able to see how nervous she was. After all, she'd taken the art class in the first place because he was in it. Rick was an art and business major and took two courses of art each semester. Lisa knew that, and a lot more, about the handsome junior in front of her. Ever since she'd been at Connors High, she'd been watching Rick from a distance. Since he was one of the most popular boys in school, and a year ahead of her, she'd never really expected much. Just to be in the same class with Rick had seemed enough.

Now she watched silently as he took out a large piece of cardboard and laid it on the worktable in front of him. As he worked he talked, taking her through the steps of mat cutting with ease and assurance. "The main thing is to keep your edges straight," he said as he deftly drew light pencil lines on the cardboard. "Then, when you use the cutter, press straight down. Don't try to go too fast. The important thing is to keep it clean and straight."

As he leaned over the cardboard, pressing the mat cutter into her material, she looked at the back of his neck. His hair, which was a deep reddish brown, curled into tiny swirls at the edge of his hairline. Lisa looked at his neck and wondered what it would be like to kiss him there. Immediately, she blushed and shook her head in embarrassment. Reminding herself that, wonderful as Rick was, he couldn't read thoughts, she forced herself

10

to concentrate on what he was saying. "So, you see, it's easy. Now you try it." Rick turned and motioned for her to come up to the table.

Lisa, not knowing how to get out of it, stepped up to the table and put her hand on the mat cutter. Rick placed his hand over hers and pressed down hard. "You've got to be boss. Treat the mat cutter as though it is a tool, not a fierce animal that might bite you," he teased.

His hand felt warm and wonderful covering hers. She felt her face flush and her heart begin to beat wildly. It was better than her dreams to be here with Rick so close beside her. She could feel his breath on her neck as he urged her, "Go ahead, don't be shy. You can do it."

Lisa forced herself to press down hard on the mat cutter and drag its sharp edge through the thick cardboard. As she neared the corner Ms. Martino called out, "Class, come here again. I forgot something."

Lisa stopped and turned to Rick, who was smiling at her in praise of her newfound skill. He said, "Go ahead. I'll finish this for you. But you did a good job." He paused and looked at her speculatively. "You're a lot stronger than you look."

Lisa blushed and practically ran to the center of the art room where Ms. Martino was talking. As she moved through the crowded classroom she knocked over a stool. Miserably embarrassed, she bent to pick the stool up, but John Reesner bent down at the same time. She bumped heads with John, and everyone laughed. Lisa stood up, feeling absolutely miserable and wishing she were anywhere in the world except this classroom. She didn't dare look over at Rick to see if he was laughing.

When Ms. Martino asked, "Are you hurt?" she shook her head no. But she *was* hurt, and there were tears in her eyes as she listened to Ms. Martino's announcement. More than the physical hurt of the bump on her forehead, she suffered an emotional hurt. Why had she let the wonderful experience with Rick turn into such a disaster? One minute she'd been standing beside him, close enough to kiss him, with his hand over hers. The next minute she'd been falling into stools and bumping heads with John. Why couldn't things work out better? Why did life always have to be so . . . sticky?

Now Ms. Martino was asking her a question. "Lisa, are you sure you haven't been hurt? You haven't heard a word I've said."

"I'm fine," Lisa answered softly, trying to keep the tears from her voice.

"Good, because you're one of the students who are getting scholarships. I was asked to pick a sophomore, a junior and a senior to attend the class. You're the sophomore, Sally's the junior and Mike's the senior. Can you attend?"

Ashamed to admit she didn't know what Ms. Martino was talking about, Lisa said, "Yes."

"Fine." Then Ms. Martino called out in a loud voice to Rick, who was picking up the pieces of cardboard he'd been working on. "Rick?"

"Yes?"

"Will you be helping Miss McGuire with the class?"

Rick grinned and answered, "I'll probably get to do the cleanup. I'm just the gopher."

Lisa wondered what a gopher was, but before anyone could ask, Ms. Martino explained. "A gopher is a slang word for the young person who runs errands and does general cleanup and odd jobs around a business. It really means go-for—that is, the one who goes for things. Many of you will start your working careers as gophers. Especially if you choose art as a way to make a living."

The bell rang then and students began leaving the classroom. Lisa, whose head still hurt, walked slowly to the door. She still didn't know why she had been chosen or what she had been chosen *for*.

Wondering if she dared ask, Lisa hesitated in the doorway for a minute. Then she realized that Rick was still cleaning up in the corner. He might think she was chasing him if she hung around the doorway. She'd seen other sophomore and freshman girls who had crushes on juniors and seniors act that way. Lisa had long ago promised herself that no matter how much she wanted to, she would never, never chase Rick Brewster. She didn't want to make a fool of herself.

She asked herself what she thought she'd done last period. If falling over stools and bumping heads with John didn't make her look foolish, then nothing would. Still, she knew she'd feel even worse if Rick ever suspected that she was crazy about him. No, it was better to ask someone else later in the day what she'd been selected to do. She hoped it was something good, since she'd already agreed to do it.

Whatever it was, it would have to wait because she was walking into her history classroom right now and history was hard enough to take all her attention. Lisa shook her head again, sat down in her seat and opened her notebook so she could begin copying the notes on the blackboard. Like some others, the history teacher had recently discovered that the third quarter was almost over. They'd proceeded carefully and slowly through the Colonial Days to the Civil War. Then, discovering that there was only a third of the year to study more than half of United States history, the teacher had begun pushing them faster and faster.

Lisa, who had a lot of trouble with dates and facts, found the increased pressure very difficult. Now, she worked quickly to get everything on the board into her notebook before the teacher began his lecture. If she took down as much as she could of what he said, she could study her notes tonight at the library. With work, she just might pass the test with a B. Lisa was aiming for a B this quarter to make up for the C-minus she'd earned the first quarter. Though it didn't come easy to her, Lisa was accustomed to making good grades. As she worked, she put all thoughts of Rick Brewster and her art class from her mind.

That evening at the library, she saw Rick again but he didn't see her. She was sitting on the side of the room, near the periodical section, looking over her notes. The minute Rick came into the library, Lisa sensed it and lifted her head from her notes.

Rick was wearing a bright blue sweatshirt with the words BREWSTER FLORIST in big blue letters. He carried a Windbreaker of the same color blue over his shoulder. Lisa watched him as he moved quickly, lightly, through the library, stopping to chat with other kids and smiling at everyone. One of the reasons that Lisa was crazy about Rick was that he really was a very friendly person. She wasn't the only girl who'd yearned to be noticed by him. Rick was popular, bright, nice and good-looking. Lisa thought he was handsome, though she knew his wide brown eyes and long nose would not fit the classic pattern of perfection.

As Rick walked from table to table Lisa hoped that

he would see her sitting alone and come over to her. In her mind, she could feel him standing beside her, his warm breath on her neck, as he had been this afternoon. Oh, if only Rick would notice her, she thought. But in her heart she knew that Rick was only being friendly today. He wasn't interested in her. She was too tall, too thin, too shy and too young to attract a boy like Rick. No, it was a doomed dream. Rick would always be out of her reach.

As though in answer to her worst thoughts, Patty Baker entered the library, looked around and walked directly toward Rick. Lisa's heart burned with feelings of sadness as she watched Patty. She was the sort of cool, poised and darling little girl that Lisa would never be. Patty never seemed to get excited. She always seemed to know what to say and exactly what to do. Her hair curled just right and her clothes were always perfect. Even her cotton blouses didn't seem to wrinkle the way other girls' did. Lisa sighed and tried to get back to her books. She was being foolish even to think about Rick. Rick had a girl and her name was Patty Baker.

During the next thirty minutes, Lisa tried very hard to force herself to concentrate on history. But every few minutes she would find that her head lifted from the book and she couldn't help looking at Rick and Patty. They looked good together, she had to admit that. For one thing, Patty was very small so she made Rick look taller than he was. For another, Patty's blond locks looked nice next to Rick's reddish-brown hair. Lisa sighed and closed her book. No doubt about it, Rick and Patty were a good couple together, and she was wasting her time trying to study when Rick was around. She picked up her jacket and started walking toward the library entrance, carefully staying on the opposite side of the room from Rick and Patty. While earlier she had hoped that Rick would see her, now she hoped he would not.

She was out the door before she heard John Reesner calling to her. She turned and found he was right behind her. "Hi, John," she said.

"Wanted to find out how your head is," John said. Then he sort of stammered, "I've got my car. Want to go for a Coke?"

Lisa was surprised that John had asked her to go for a Coke. She'd never paid much attention to John and they weren't really friends. Still, John was in two of her classes this year, so she knew him slightly.

She said yes and followed him to his car. It was a small, rusty VW beetle. Lisa felt tall and awkward as she climbed into the front seat. She laughed and asked, "How do you manage? You're even taller than I am."

"I'm used to it," John answered. Then he asked, "I'm six feet two. How tall are you, Lisa?"

"Five feet nine," she lied.

"Really? I would have thought you were close to six feet."

For the second time that day, Lisa wished the earth would swallow her. She was really about five feet ten and a half, but she knew she looked taller because she was so thin. But six feet? She must really look tall and skinny. As she searched for something to say, she thought of Patty Baker. Patty was probably about five feet five and she always knew what to say. Worse yet, Lisa knew that Rick was exactly her own height. Why did all the cute guys have to be short? All this was going through her mind while she searched for something to say to John. Finally, she asked, "John, did you know that you might not be through growing? I am, though. Girls finish a lot faster than boys."

"Yeah," John said. Then he grinned. "If I get too tall for it, I'll sell you my bug cheap."

Lisa laughed and leaned back against the VW seat. She decided that John was a nice guy. Too bad he wasn't her type, but he wasn't. Lisa knew that John was just as shy and quiet as she was. She wanted a man who was more outgoing—more like Rick, she thought sadly. Thinking of Rick made her more silent than usual.

When they were inside the booth at the coffee shop where they'd gone for a Coke, Lisa asked, "Do you know what Ms. Martino was talking about today?"

"What do you mean?"

"After we bumped our heads, she said I had a scholarship. But I don't know what she was talking about. Do you?" Lisa waited for an answer.

"Hey," John said in a worried voice, "are you sure you're all right? Maybe you got a concussion or something."

"No, I'm fine," Lisa said. She didn't tell him that she had been too upset to listen well. "I just never did catch what she was talking about. Did you?"

John was still looking at her strangely as he said, "You are supposed to go to a flower-arranging class at the Women's Club. The manager of Brewster Florist will teach you how to arrange flowers. The people at the club will buy their flowers, but you get yours free. It's a scholarship."

"When is the class?" Lisa's heart was beating fast again. Would this be the chance she needed to get acquainted with Rick?

"There are three sessions. Tomorrow night is the first. I forget when." Then John smiled and added, "I wasn't the one who was picked to go, so I didn't pay much attention to the time."

"I'll ask Ms. Martino tomorrow," Lisa said. Then she added, "Thanks, John. Thanks for the Coke, too."

"Would you like to go out with me Friday night?" John asked. His face was red and he seemed to blurt out the words in one big rush.

Lisa bent the straw in her glass, twisting it into a small snaillike circle. She didn't know what to answer. Except for one dreadful party in junior high, she hadn't really dated. She was relieved that someone had finally asked her out. But John? Somehow, she'd never thought of John as a possibility. He wasn't so bad, but he seemed so . . . ordinary. She looked up and saw the anxious, tense expression on his face as he waited for an answer. Who did she think she was anyway? She was pretty ordinary herself, wasn't she? Lisa took a deep breath and smiled. "I think that would be nice, John. What time will you pick me up?"

2

Lisa dressed for the course in flower arranging three times before she decided to wear Levi's and her lilac sweater. She wasn't sure that Rick would pay any attention to her, but she wanted to look as nice as possible. She sighed as she brushed her long, straight black hair. For perhaps the hundredth time, she wished for regular blue eyes and brown hair. If only her skin weren't so white and her eyes such a funny color of gray-blue, she'd be happy. Black hair wasn't so bad, she supposed, but her looks were so different that people often turned and stared at her.

Ever since she'd been a little girl, she'd known that she was going to look like her father. Sam Kelly was six foot four and a handsome, smiling man. Lisa frowned as she thought of her father's laughter when he said, "Poor little colleen, she looks just like me. Spitting image, as we say in the old country."

That had been when she'd been younger. Now they didn't talk much about how she looked. Sometimes her mother seemed anxious when they shopped for clothing, but she knew both her parents were trying hard not to say anything to give her an inferiority complex. Lisa sighed and touched a bit of blusher to her high cheekbones. She didn't have a complex, she thought. She was just facing facts. The facts were that she was too tall, too thin and too funny-looking. She sighed again and brushed her lips with deep plum lip gloss. Her friend Angela had helped her pick the color out, insisting that it highlighted her eyes.

Lisa looked in the mirror with a worried expression on her face as she remember that Angela had said she looked stunning in the plum-colored lip gloss. Stunning —that was what you said to a plain girl when you wanted to cheer her up. No one ever called her pretty when they looked at her high cheekbones and wide-set eyes. No, they used words like dramatic or stunning when all she really wanted was to be a regular, pretty sixteen-year-old girl.

Finally, she was satisfied that she'd done the best she could and she went into the living room to say goodbye. Her mother and father were working the crossword puzzle together and barely looked up when Lisa came in. She told them she'd be back before ten and started for the front door. Her mother said automatically, "Take your raincoat. It's wet outside."

"Miserable March weather," her father added. "Better wear boots."

Lisa didn't even bother to answer as she threw her Windbreaker over her shoulders and ran for the car. One good thing about having long, straight hair was that it wouldn't look too bad even if it did get a little wet. Of course, she didn't want to look like a drenched rat, so she was happy her folks had let her use the car. Besides, she'd spent so much time getting ready that she was late for the flower-arranging class.

As she pulled into the Women's Club parking lot she realized she didn't know where to go. Her mother, who was an accountant, never went to that sort of social group. For that matter, Lisa hadn't belonged to a club since she left Girl Scouts in the seventh grade. Why was she going to this class tonight? Did she really want to spend three evenings learning something as simple as putting flowers in a bowl?

But Lisa knew she was just kidding herself if she pretended she was at the meeting because she wanted to know about flowers. She was there because Rick Brewster would be there. Taking a deep breath, Lisa entered the Women's Club building and followed the sound of voices down the hall.

She looked inside the door of a large room and the first person she saw was Rick. Knowing she was in the right place didn't make her entrance any easier for Lisa. She felt awkward and out of place as she stood in the doorway, wondering what to do next. There were about thirty people in the room and most of them seemed to be older than her own parents. She looked for the other two students from the art class and saw one of them at the end of a long table.

Shyly, Lisa started walking toward Sally, who was from her class. But before she could get more than five feet into the room, a short, red-haired woman in a bright red smock called out, "You must be the other student."

Lisa changed her direction and walked toward the woman in the red smock. When she got a little closer, the woman said, "I'm Molly. Molly McGuire. You can work right here, beside me." Molly pointed to a small space to her right. Standing beside Molly, she realized that the woman was very short. Molly apparently noticed the difference also, because she turned to Lisa and said in a cheerful voice. "My, it must be wonderful to be so tall. You can reach all the high places, can't you?"

Lisa blushed, hoping that Rick hadn't heard what Molly had said. She herself could think of nothing to say, so she looked down at the stack of materials in front of her.

Molly, who was at the end of the table, cleared her voice and called down to the group, "All right. Let's begin."

Lisa looked around for Rick, trying not to raise her eyes or crane her neck, but she couldn't see him. In fact, the only person she saw that she knew was Sally at the end of the table. She wasn't sure where the third student who had a scholarship was. Lisa forced herself to stop thinking about Rick and start concentrating on the lesson in front of her.

Molly was talking about the way a flower arrangement should reflect good design. As she talked she put some green foam into a small white container and began stuffing dark green leaves into the foam. "This is laurel," Molly said. "Here in the Northeast, we use laurel for the background a lot. It's cheap and easy to find. Of course, it's illegal to pick laurel in Massachusetts, so we have to get it from a dealer in New York. He delivers it in bundles two times a week." Then Molly opened her hands wide and said, "Big bundles—bales, really." She added, "One requirement for being a florist is strength; another is stamina." She laughed. "I'm strong and I can work long hours without falling down, so I worked my way up from gopher to manager in just a few years. Of course, you folks don't want jobs in the florist business. You just want to learn how to put flowers in a bowl and make them pretty, don't you?" As she finished the question she used her hands to imitate the shape of leaves she'd added in the bowl. She asked, "What have I done here?"

The room was silent and Lisa was a little surprised that the grown-ups seemed as hesitant about answering as she was. Molly turned to Lisa and asked, "What have I done here?"

Lisa blushed again, hoping that she would give the right answer and hoping that Rick wouldn't think she was a dumbbell if she gave the wrong one. "You made a circle—a mound of leaves," Lisa said.

"Good girl!" Molly said enthusiastically. Then she turned to the class and continued her demonstration, pointing out that the leaves were shaped so that the tallest part was exactly in the center of the bowl.

As she watched Molly, Lisa decided that she was a nice woman. In some ways, she reminded Lisa of Ms. Martino, the art teacher who'd chosen her to come here. Both women were full of enthusiasm and energy. Both obviously loved their work. Of course, Ms. Martino was graceful and glamorous-looking, while Molly was short and sort of dumpy. Lisa decided that both women were about thirty-five and, since neither wore a wedding ring, both were single. Funny how two women could have so much in common and be so different. Ms. Martino always had bright red fingernails and wore expensive clothes, even to teach in an art class. Molly looked as though she hadn't thought anything at all about her appearance. But she was nice, Lisa decided. Very nice.

Molly was selecting flowers now and breaking the stems before she put them into the arrangement, fastening them to the green foam. Lisa watched carefully as the small vase seemed to fill with flowers almost by itself. All the while she worked, Molly kept up a running patter, making jokes and pointing out the basic rules of design. Once, she made a joke about Rick, saying that he was handsome but his father was even better looking.

By this time Lisa had located Rick, who was standing behind a stout woman down at the end of the table. When Molly made the crack about his looks, Lisa looked up at Rick's face to see if he was hurt. He was laughing and seemed to think it was just fine. In fact, he answered back by saying, "Don't let her kid you. It's my little brother she's after; he's the best-looking of all."

Lisa found herself laughing along with the others. Suddenly, she was very glad she'd come to the class. Even though Rick hadn't really said hello to her, it was wonderful to be a part of his world. Lisa knew that Rick spent a lot of time working at his dad's florist shop. She had heard that he was studying art and business so that he could go to work with his father when he graduated from high school. Lisa wondered if that was true and decided it was something she could ask him sometime. After all, now that he'd helped her in class and she was coming to a course sponsored by his family business, it would be all right to talk to him. That wouldn't be chasing him, to ask something about his future plans. Lisa found herself daydreaming about an imaginary conversation she might start with Rick tomorrow in class.

But it wasn't long before the daydream ended and the work began. Molly, after showing everyone her floral arrangement, said, "O.K. Now get to work."

Rick and Molly quickly put bunches of pompom chrysanthemums on the table. There were buckets of laurel leaves standing on the floor between every six or ten people. Lisa reached out for the small white vase in front of her and then tucked a piece of green foam into it. She saw that Rick wasn't doing an arrangement. He was carrying a pitcher of water around the table, pouring water into each little bowl.

Lisa's fingers were trembling as she reached for her first piece of laurel. Somehow, it seemed very important to do a perfect arrangement. She looked for a branch of laurel that had no holes or dusty spots on the leaves and quickly broke off a few small branches. Then she began putting the leaves into the foam, carefully following the mounded shape that Molly had demonstrated. After the first few movements, her hands stopped trembling and she began enjoying herself. Funny, she'd never really thought about flowers before. They had a few marigolds and geraniums growing between the vegetables at home, but no one ever did more than pick them and stick them in a vase. As Lisa worked she promised herself that this summer she'd ask for more and different flowers in the garden. She was sure her folks would agree to anything if she'd promise to do the weeding.

As she thought about it Lisa realized that she was the only one in her family who really cared much about the garden anyway. The rest of them only worked in the garden long enough to guarantee a good crop of tomatoes and corn. It was she who nursed the other crops, covering the lettuce and staking the beans to keep them growing at the right rate.

"You're good at that," a voice behind her said.

Lisa jumped as Rick, who was behind her, brought the pitcher of water around to fill her vase. Her arm jiggled against his but he didn't spill the water. "Steady there," he teased. "Compliments really go to your head, don't they?"

"I don't get many," Lisa whispered. The minute she said that, she was sorry. Now he would think she was a total loser. Oh, if only she didn't say the wrong thing all the time! Lisa looked helplessly at the back of Rick's head as he moved on to the next person. Then she turned back to the flower arrangement in front of her.

She was trying to decide whether she needed one more yellow pompom when Molly said, "Now, stop right where you are. Let's take a look at what you're doing." She picked Lisa's arrangement up and held it up to the class.

"This one is perfect," Molly said. "Notice the way the yellows and oranges balance each other. And look at the way she's built a mound of color. No holes in this design. It's a simple, clean arrangement. The sort we sell in the shop for ten dollars every day."

Lisa smiled with pleasure. It was the second time someone had singled her work out as an example of excellence. She looked at her own design and decided she was quite pleased with it. In fact, she had enjoyed working with the flowers as much as anything else she'd ever done with art. Wouldn't it be wonderful if Rick noticed how talented she was and asked her to help him out sometime in the flower shop? She looked around for Rick, to see if he was watching. Her pleasure dimmed a bit when she saw that he was busy gathering up the laurel branches and stuffing the remains into a large cardboard carton. She could tell by the way he worked that Rick wasn't very interested in the simple designs the class was producing. He moved quickly and efficiently, cleaning and collecting materials. Lisa watched him for a while, enjoying the chance to adore him from afar without worrying about what anyone would think. It never occurred to her that anyone would notice.

But as Molly dismissed the class, telling them all that they were very talented, she added in a soft voice to Lisa, "Next time, honey, don't wear your heart on your sleeve."

Lisa looked down at the cheerful redhead in embarrassment. She would have liked to deny that she'd been thinking of Rick, but the older woman's friendly face and soft smile made it impossible. Lisa asked, "It shows that much?"

Molly chuckled. "I'm not sure he knows, but you've got one of those honest, open faces that show a lot. Don't ever get in a poker game." With that she laughed and said, "Don't let me bug you, kid. I'm harmless. What did you say your name was?"

"Lisa. Lisa Kelly."

Molly nodded her head. "Lisa Kelly and Molly McGuire. We sound like a couple of characters in an Irish comedy, don't we?"

Lisa nodded her head. Molly looked like the sort of person one thought of as being of Irish extraction. She was short, freckle-faced and red-haired. But Lisa knew her own tall, dark looks were also traditionally Irish. Her father had once told her that it was believed that many centuries ago their ancestors had mixed with

Spanish seafarers and that explained the "black Irish," as he called himself.

As she helped Molly clean up the supplies in front of them Lisa realized that she'd enjoyed the little woman's lesson very much. She told her so.

Molly, obviously pleased, said, "I love flowers. All my life I've wanted to work with them. And that's what I do, so I'm a happy woman."

Lisa believed her. She wondered if she herself would ever find anything that would make her happy. Oh, she knew she had a good life right now. She did well in school. She had a nice family. She had all the things a sixteen-year-old girl was supposed to have—except a boyfriend. But she knew that she spent a lot of time worrying. She worried about her looks, about her grades and about her future. She also spent a lot of time worrying about what Rick Brewster thought of her. Worst of all, she knew that was silly because Rick didn't think about her at all.

As she left the flower-arranging lesson she looked around, hoping to be able to say good-bye to Rick, but he was talking to Sally. Lisa just didn't have the nerve to go over and break into their conversation. She stood in the doorway for a moment, wishing she were a different, braver sort of person, and then she turned and left.

3

When Lisa woke the next morning, her first thought was of Rick. Would he be friendly when she saw him in school? Not that Rick wasn't always friendly to everyone; he usually said hello and smiled, but Lisa hoped for more. Perhaps the flower-arranging class would be a stepping-stone to romance.

Lisa smiled at her silly dreams and got out of bed. She shivered as her bare feet hit the cold wooden floor. Slipping into her fuzzy slippers, she pulled on her robe and walked down the hall to the bathroom. As she showered she found herself dreaming of Rick again. Shaking her head to clear her thoughts, she reminded herself that Rick Brewster never thought about her. Lisa stepped out of the shower and rubbed herself briskly with a large orange towel. It just wasn't fair, she thought. Why did she have to be crazy about someone who didn't even know she was alive?

Even though she was convinced it was hopeless, Lisa dressed with care, selecting her prettiest blue sweater and best blue slacks to wear to school. She brushed her long, heavy black hair back behind her ears and pinned two bright blue combs into her hair. Turning sideways and holding a hand mirror to the back of her head, she could see that the blue combs made her black hair seem shinier and glossier than ever.

As Lisa finished dressing, paying special attention to her makeup and trying eye shadow twice before deciding against it, her little brother Eddie pounded on the bathroom door. Soon he began kicking, and her mother yelled from upstairs, "Lisa, get out of the bathroom right now!"

Lisa sighed, put on lipstick and left the bathroom. As she passed Eddie in the hallway, he said, "Hi, ugly. Why do you spend so long in there? It don't do no good."

"Doesn't do any good," Lisa corrected automatically. She was used to her nine-year-old brother's complaints in the mornings. Usually he was a good enough kid, but they often fought over the use of the bathroom as they were getting ready for school. And Lisa had to admit that Eddie often had to wait.

This morning, Eddie seemed very angry. As she descended the stairs and walked toward the kitchen, he yelled after her, "Ugly! Ugly! Ugly!"

Lisa's face was burning, but she tried to look as dignified and uninvolved as possible as she walked into the kitchen. She didn't see any sense in getting everyone stirred up by fighting back at Eddie. Besides that, it bothered her a lot to have Eddie call her ugly. She was afraid he was right. Was she really ugly?

As she nodded to her mother and went to the toaster

to put in two slices of bread she could feel her lower lip tremble and her eyes begin to fill with tears. Darn that Eddie! she thought. It would be awful if she began to cry now. One of the things that Lisa hated most in the world was to cry. And part of the reason she hated to cry was that it made her white skin turn red and blotchy.

Eddie was still yelling the same word from the top of the stairs. Her mother looked up from her newspaper and said, "You two at it again?"

"That's not fair," Lisa protested. "He's the one who's yelling. Not me."

Her mother smiled and said, "But you're the one who spent forty-five minutes in the bathroom." Then she turned and called up the stairs to her son, "I don't want to hear another word from you. Not one."

Lisa and her mother waited for a moment. There was silence and then the sound of the bathroom door closing. Lisa took her toast out of the toaster and buttered it lightly. Then she poured herself a glass of milk and sat down across the table from her mother. Mrs. Kelly asked, "Is that all you're going to eat?"

"It's a good breakfast," Lisa said quickly.

"You don't eat enough," her mother complained. "Young girl like you needs healthy food. Plenty of energy. You're too thin."

Sam Kelly looked up from his paper and said in a quiet voice, "Sue, let her alone. She's not too thin, she's just right."

Lisa looked down at the toast in front of her. Tears were swimming in her eyes now. One plopped onto the plate, just splashing the corner of her toast. She knew she wasn't going to be able to eat a bite of breakfast, and she knew that would make her mother very unhappy. If her mother began to nag her, her father would probably try to defend her again. Lisa could see the whole scene in her mind, and it made her feel just awful. She didn't know what was worse—her mother's obvious concern because of her tall, thin looks or her father's anxious insistence that she was all right.

"What are you crying about?" her mother asked. Sue Kelly's voice sounded angry.

"I'm not crying," Lisa said.

"You're crying," her mother countered. "You're crying all over your toast. What in the world for?"

"Soggy toast isn't good for you," her father joked.

But Lisa wasn't in the mood for jokes, and she certainly didn't want to tell her parents what she was crying about. She knew they would both think she was silly if she told them she was crying because she was ugly. Besides, she was feeling so bad that she didn't really want to talk to anyone at all. She just wanted to get out of the house before something happened to make her feel worse. She put her napkin on the table and stood up.

"Sit down," her mother commanded.

"I'm not hungry," Lisa answered and started for the door.

"You heard your mother," Sam Kelly roared.

Lisa stopped and turned, then moved slowly back to the chair. Sam Kelly was a soft-spoken man. He never nagged her as her mother often did, but Lisa knew he was angry now. She looked down at the soggy toast, and tears began to drop out of her eyes at an alarming rate.

Her father said in a softer voice, "You must apologize to your mother, Lisa. She asked you what was wrong and you didn't want to answer. Maybe that was your right. But you have no right to leave the table after your mother tells you to sit still."

"I'm sorry, Mother."

"Apology accepted," her mother said briskly. "Now I'm going to try again. Lisa, what is wrong with you? Why are you so moody? Why were you crying? What's going on with you? You've always been such a sweet little girl."

"Mother, I'm not a little girl. I'm almost six feet tall."

Her mother asked sharply, "Is that what you're crying about? Because you're tall?"

"No." But in a way, that was part of it, wasn't it? She just couldn't talk about her feelings to her mother and father. She didn't even have the words to tell them how desperate she felt about the way she looked. Nor could she ever admit how much she wanted Rick Brewster to think she was pretty, to notice her. She looked up from her plate and said, "Mother, I've really got to go. I'm going to be late for school."

Her mother sighed and said, "All right, Lisa. I can't force you to discuss things with us. But I have a feeling you're worrying too much about things over which you have no control." She stopped for a moment before she added in a softer voice, "Lisa, there are worse things in this world than being tall. A lot of beautiful women are tall."

"I know, Mother."

"Besides, you are not six feet tall! As usual, you are exaggerating. And if you'd eat a little more, you wouldn't be so thin. You might not even look—"

"Sue," Sam Kelly interrupted. "Lisa's worried about being late. Is it all right if she goes now?"

Her mother frowned and said, "Of course. Lisa, I

hope you have a good day. Try not to worry so much. And I'll be needing the car tonight for a late meeting. Is that all right?"

"I have a date," Lisa said. When her parents looked at her in amazement, she added, "You don't need to look so surprised. It isn't my first date, you know." She hoped that they wouldn't point out it was her first date in over a year. She felt bad enough about herself without that.

But both of her parents tried to cover their surprise quickly. Her mother said, "That's nice, Lisa. Who are you going out with? And where?"

"John Reesner. He's in my art class at school. I'm not sure where we're going. But you don't have to worry. John is the sensible type." She didn't add that she thought John was a little dull.

"We don't worry about you," her father said. "You're a wonderful girl, Lisa. We're always proud of you."

Lisa winced. When her father said those things, she could never decide whether he meant them or was just making them up to make her feel better about herself. Either way, it was embarrassing.

As Lisa left her home and began the walk to school she found herself wondering how things had gone so wrong so quickly. She'd felt fine when she got up that morning, and within thirty minutes she'd been fighting with her brother and her mother. Worse yet, she'd cried all over her toast. Now she was on her way to school with a red face and no breakfast.

Her friend Angela was waiting on the corner, pounding her arms with her mittened hands against the cold spring air. "You're late," Angela said. "I'm almost frozen stiff."

"Sorry," Lisa apologized automatically.

"How was it?" Angela asked.

"What?"

"How was your flower class? Did you get to talk to Rick?" Angela asked.

Lisa flushed. She wished she had never told Angela about her crush on Rick. Angela was a good friend, but she talked a lot and always asked a lot of questions. Lisa often thought it would be nice if she and Angela could trade some qualities. She wished she weren't as shy, and it would be good for Angela if she weren't quite so outspoken.

"Flower arranging was fun. I liked it a lot," Lisa answered.

"Then why were you crying?" Angela asked.

Again, Lisa flushed red. "I wasn't crying, I have a cold," she lied. She hoped that would keep Angela quiet for a while.

"Did you talk to Rick?" Angela asked.

"No, I didn't," Lisa answered. Then she added, "Look, Angie, could we talk about something else? I have a cold and don't feel very well."

"You've been crying," Angela accused.

Lisa could tell that her friend's feelings were hurt, but there wasn't much she could do about it. What was wrong this morning? she asked herself. It seemed as though everything she touched turned bad. What was she doing wrong?

As though she read her mind, Angela said, "Your trouble is that you have an inferiority complex, Lisa. You just don't know how to put yourself across as a stunning, attractive human being. You've got to learn to glow and glitter. Shine, Lisa, shine! Then Rick will notice you."

"Please," Lisa wailed. "I told you I didn't feel good. Could we just get off this subject?"

"Sure," Angela said. "I was just trying to help. But you obviously don't know you need help."

Lisa heard the hurt in Angela's voice. She said, "Angie, I know you're trying to help me, but sometimes you sound like my mother. I'm just not up to it. O.K.?"

Angela didn't even answer her. The two girls walked the rest of the way to school in silence. In fact, Angela seemed to be making a big effort to keep a few steps ahead of Lisa. And Lisa, who really didn't feel well by then, began to lag behind.

By the time they came to the steps of Connors High School, the friends were almost ten feet apart. Lisa watched the back of Angela's body move quickly up the stairs. She called to her friend, "See you at lunch," but Angela did not turn around.

After a beginning like that, school could only improve matters. Lisa was actually happy to go into her classes where she would have to study and pay attention to the teacher. It got her mind off herself and her own problems. She enjoyed her morning classes, and by the time she went to art she was a little more relaxed.

Rick was in art class, working on a large painting he'd started as part of his independent project. Lisa looked at him when she entered the class and he looked up just at that time. Lisa felt her face flush but she said, "Hi, Rick, how are you?"

"Fine," Rick answered. "Did you have fun last night?"

"I loved it," Lisa answered honestly. "I think working with flowers is just great."

"Good." Rick smiled at her. For a minute her eyes met his warm brown ones and she felt that old familiar flutter in her stomach. When he smiled like that, she felt as though someone were turning on sunshine. He really was a wonderful, wonderful person, she told herself.

Lisa tried to think of something clever to say. If only she had a quick mind and tongue, she could think of words to capture Rick's interest. As it was, she stumbled as she said, "I'll be there again next week. Will you?"

"Sure," Rick said. "It's my job. Or part of my job. Most of the time I help around the shop or drive the delivery truck."

"Do you like that?"

"Which?" Rick teased. "The cleaning or the driving or hanging out at the Women's Club?"

"Which do you like best?" Lisa asked. She felt she was being silly and wondered if he could tell she was just asking questions to keep him talking to her longer. Would Rick think she was just a silly sophomore?

"I like it all," Rick said. "It's work and they pay me." Then he turned back to his painting, dismissing her.

Lisa stood there, feeling awkward and silly but unable to find the right thing to say before she left. She wanted desperately to make it seem casual and unimportant, and at the same time she wanted to hold on to him as long as she could. She spoke to his back because he was facing his painting now. "I like your painting. The ships are nice."

"Thanks," Rick said.

Lisa felt waves of embarrassment flood over her. She was obviously being dismissed. Rick didn't seem to want to talk anymore, and yet she didn't seem to be able to go away. She waited, hoping he would take pity on her awkwardness and turn to say something to help her out. But Rick kept right on painting while she stood on the sidelines, watching him.

Finally, after what seemed like hours. she managed to croak, "See you later."

Rick turned briefly and flashed his wonderful smile at her. "Sure, Lisa," he said.

Lisa turned and went to her own work area as quickly as she could. At her own desk, she got out her materials with trembling fingers and tried to go to work. But all the time she was brushing color over the blank white paper, she was going over her conversation with Rick. Had she made a fool of herself again? Did Rick know she was crazy about him? If so, what would he think of her? And, worst of all, would Rick try to avoid her after this?

By the time class was over, she'd convinced herself that Rick would probably think she was the biggest ninny in the world. When he walked by her without even nodding his head in her direction, she knew she had been right.

Everything about the day had been a total disaster. She was pretty sure that her date with John that evening would be more of the same.

4

Lisa's date with John Reesner wasn't a disaster, just dull. John arrived at exactly seven o'clock and drove her to a movie which began at seven fifteen. By nine thirty, they were staring at each other over two Cokes. Lisa yawned and John, apparently eager for something to say, asked, "Are you tired?"

Surprised to find that it was true, Lisa answered yes. She said, "I guess I didn't get enough sleep last night. Sorry I'm such dull company."

"You're not dull," John assured her. "But I'll take you home if you want." His voice sounded almost eager, and Lisa was pretty sure that he was as glad to cut the evening short as she was. John seemed to have a lot of trouble finding anything to say to her, and she certainly wasn't helping him.

If her parents were surprised to find her at home by

ten, they didn't say anything. Her mother looked up from her book and asked, "Have fun?"

"The movie was good," Lisa answered. She went into the kitchen, cut herself a slice of cake and poured a glass of milk. Then she went to her room to read. But even after she was settled down with a good book, she found that she was tired and listless. Instead of reading, Lisa stared out the window at the full moon and dreamed of Rick.

What was Rick doing right this minute? Was he out with Patty? Or was he home watching television? Or reading? Lisa spun a little story to herself about Rick sitting by his own window, staring at the same moon and dreaming of her. If only that were true. If only Rick Brewster were dreaming of her. Wouldn't it be wonderful if he were to call her on the telephone right now?

Then Lisa did something she hadn't done since seventh grade. She remembered a seventh-grade slumber party where all the girls had tried to do experiments with ESP and mental messages. They'd worked all that year to get people to call them on the telephone or to figure out who it 'was when the phone rang. Lisa remembered that for a while she'd been quite convinced she was psychic. She had been able to guess who was calling a lot of the time. Of course, it was usually Angela or Mary Ann in those days.

Feeling silly but wanting desperately to believe it would work, Lisa closed her eyes and tried to conjure up a vision of Rick. She worked a long time to see if she could get a clear picture of Rick in her mind. At times she could fasten his warm brown eyes on the screen of her mind. At other times she could capture his wonderful smile. Then she was able to project the whole image of the back of his head and neck, the soft brown curls she'd wanted to kiss. Quickly, before the image faded, she sent Rick a message: "Call me. Love me. Love me."

For a moment, the feeling was so strong that she almost expected the telephone to ring. Lisa sat curled in her chair, eyes closed, fists clenched, and waited. She waited a long time before she gave up and went to bed. Even then, she held on to the dream and a feeling of expectancy. Maybe, just maybe, Rick had received her message. Maybe, in time, he would act on it.

If Rick had received any psychic message, he certainly didn't show any signs of it when she saw him in school on Monday. As always, he was friendly and had a few warm words for Lisa before he went back to work on his painting. Lisa, still feeling silly about last night and at the same time feeling hopeful, hung around and talked to him just as long as she dared. Rick didn't seem to mind talking a bit, but he didn't seem very interested in her either.

During the next week, Lisa looked for signs of interest on Rick's part but had to admit that she saw none at all. Rick was friendly and that was all. Nevertheless, Lisa wanted to keep as much contact with him as possible, so she went back to the flower-arranging class.

Once in the class, she forgot that it was only because of Rick that she was there. She looked at the lovely daffodils and irises in the bucket in front of her and said, "Oh, they're lovely! Will we use these?"

Molly's eyes lighted up as she saw Lisa and she said, "Yes, Lisa, they're for you to use. Of course, you'll use a lot of pinks too."

"Pinks?"

"Carnations," Molly explained. "Here's Rick with the pink carnations right now."

Lisa watched Rick carry a very long cardboard box into the room. He put the box of flowers down in the middle of the table in front of Molly and said, "There's another box in the truck. I'll be right back." Then he stopped for a moment, looked up and said, "Hi, Lisa. How's it going?"

"Hi, Rick," Lisa said. Then she took a deep breath and asked, "Would you like me to help you?" Her heart was beating fast as she waited for the answer.

But Rick didn't answer at all. In fact, he didn't seem to hear her as he turned and walked back to the doorway of the Women's Club.

Lisa's face must have shown her disappointment, because Molly said, "He's a hard worker. He doesn't always hear things when he's concentrating. He didn't mean to be rude."

"Oh, Rick could never be rude," Lisa said quickly in his defense.

Molly's eyes were twinkling as she said softly, "Got it bad, huh, kid? Well, you can help me if you want."

At Molly's direction, Lisa lifted the long-stemmed pink carnations from the box and placed them in the buckets of water on the table. When Rick brought the second box in, he helped her get the rest of the flowers ready for the class.

When they were finished, Rick said to Molly, "O.K. if I go get a hamburger? I'll be back fast."

"Take an hour," Molly said. "There won't be anything to do for a while. I'm giving a lecture on design before we do this one."

Lisa was disappointed that Rick wasn't around during the first part of the class, but she had an idea she learned more. Molly talked for quite a while about the basic designs used in flower arranging. As she explained the standard shapes and the use of color for balance, Lisa found she was really very interested. The flowers, with their clear, bright colors, kept drawing her eyes.

Once, she wanted to touch the long purple irises whose petals flopped down, looking a lot like the soft plush of a puppy's ears. Lisa smiled at the thought of a purple puppy dog. It would have to be a basset or dachshund with long floppy ears. Or maybe the irises were more like velvet flags—the sort that knights carried in the old days of chivalry.

Lisa was surprised that she was thinking such romantic and imaginative thoughts. Usually, she was very matter-of-fact and practical. Even as a child, she had preferred realistic stories to fairy tales or fantasy. But working with flowers seemed to spark another side of her nature, and she enjoyed it.

She especially enjoyed working with these lovely long-stemmed spring flowers. This time, their containers were shallow, square bowls, and a wire-mesh base was used to fasten the flowers into place. Lisa chose a beautiful purple iris as her tallest and most important flower in the arrangement. Then she placed a bright yellow daffodil on each side of the iris. One of the daffodils was slightly shorter than the other; Molly had said it was important not to make the tall flowers look like soldiers lined up for battle. Then Lisa used the bright pink carnations to fill in her triangular design. Unlike most of the others, Lisa did not use short daffodils or irises to balance the color. Instead, she she used some taller carnations. When she had finished, her arrangement was mostly pink, with just one iris and two daffodils. She stepped back and looked at it anxiously. Had she done right?

Lisa looked at her own design for a long time. It seemed beautiful to her. Then she walked slowly up and down the long table where the others were working on their arrangements. Some were still struggling to get the straight, tall flowers into the pot. One or two had ignored the directions completely and lined their flowers up at almost even heights. One man had put four tall flowers one at each corner of his vase and then filled in the center with shorter ones. Lisa was amazed that so many of the arrangements were either dull or disturbing. She found some she liked but none she liked any better than her own. She wondered if she was getting conceited. It was a new feeling to think she was the best at something. But she liked the feeling, she liked it very much.

When Molly picked her arrangement as one of the examples, she wasn't surprised but she was pleased. It really did feel good to be the best at something and she found herself thinking sadly that next week would be the last class session. She decided to ask Molly about books she could read. Maybe this summer, when she would have flowers of her own, she could continue with this hobby.

"You're the star again tonight," Rick's voice came from behind her shoulder.

Lisa jumped a little bit, then turned and smiled at him. "I love it," she said.

"Being the star?" he asked.

"That too," she admitted. "But I meant I loved arranging flowers. Don't you?"

"I like flowers," Rick said. "But I don't have the

natural ability that you and Molly have. My arrangements are fine; I've learned a lot, of course. But yours are special. You're talented."

Lisa's face glowed with pleasure at the compliment. She could think of nothing to say except "Thank you."

She watched Rick as he worked picking up the flower stems and trash on the tables. She wondered if he'd really meant what he'd said or if he was just being polite. It would be nice to think that she did have a special talent. In school, she'd always been one of those students who worked hard for Bs and an occasional A. Nothing wrong, but nothing all that right, either. But working with flowers was something she loved to do, and maybe she really was especially good at it.

She carried her arrangement home with pride. Her parents were pleased and impressed with it. Her mother said, "Would you like to put it in the living room or in your own room?"

"Put it in the living room," her little brother Eddie said. "I'm not allowed to go into Lisa's room."

Lisa left the flowers in the living room, and all week long the Kelly family members seemed to enjoy them. The day before her last class, her mother said, "I'm afraid we'll have to throw your lovely arrangement out today. It's a shame."

"I'll try and bring another one home tomorrow," Lisa said. She really was pleased that her family seemed to enjoy the flowers so much. She was also pleased that Rick, though he clearly wasn't interested in her romantically, was so friendly at school. Things seemed to be going well, for a change.

For the last class, Molly showed them a selection of specialty arrangements, using special types of containers. There were baby's booties to fill with carnations and mums, and lovely lacy baskets for weddings. There was even one frame for a casket arrangement. The class members had to select a container that they wanted to buy. Molly said to Lisa and the other students, "You may choose any one that costs less than ten dollars. It's part of your scholarship."

Lisa couldn't decide whether to take a simple white vase for roses and carnations or a cute little cup in the shape of a baseball for her little brother Eddie. She stood for a long time, trying to make up her mind or hoping that someone would buy one and she'd be left with the other.

"Can't make up your mind?" Molly asked.

"I ought to bring something to my folks, but I'd kind of like the baseball cup for my little brother. I never do anything for him," Lisa explained.

"Take both," Molly said. "You'll be able to do two in the time it takes most of these turkeys to do one."

"Oh, I couldn't," Lisa said. "But maybe I could buy the other one."

"Take them both," Molly said. "I'll send you a bill."

Knowing that Molly would never send her a bill but unable to argue any longer, Lisa took the simple little vase and the baseball cup back to her working place.

She had a wonderful time filling Eddie's cup with bright yellow and orange mums. But she loved working with the wonderful lacy ferns and red roses more than anything she'd ever done. When the class was over, Lisa felt so happy and excited that she almost forgot to ask Molly about the books.

"Tell you what," Molly said as she thought about Lisa's question. "Come to our open house on Palm Sunday. I'll show you around and loan you a couple of my books. The stuff they have in the library is no good.

Not practical in the Northeast. Everything they show calls for orchids or some other tropical flower that costs twenty dollars a stem."

"I'd love to come to the open house," Lisa said.

"You can bring a friend," Molly said. "It's open to the public."

Lisa decided to invite Angela to go with her to the open house that Sunday. It would be a way of making up with her old friend, and it would be easier to go into Brewster Florist with a friend than alone.

On Sunday, she spent a long, long time dressing. Once, her brother Eddie knocked on the door and asked politely if he could come in for a Band-Aid. Ever since she'd brought him the flower arrangement with the baseball cup, Eddie had been nice to her.

Once inside the bathroom, Eddie got his Band-Aid and then stood for a long time watching Lisa put on makeup. As she applied a coat of liquid mascara Eddie asked, "Do you think that stuff helps?"

Instead of getting mad at him, Lisa turned and smiled. "I hope so. Now scram."

For once Eddie didn't tell her she was ugly, and her mother told her she looked very nice. When she picked up Angela, her friend said, "You look great. Maybe Rick will notice."

Lisa felt her stomach knot with fear. She said, "Angela, promise me you won't say anything to Rick."

"You mean you don't want me to talk to him at all?" Angela asked innocently. "You mean you got all dressed up in your white slacks and pink sweater and now we can't even talk to him?"

"Don't say anything . . . you know, anything personal."

Angela looked as though she were going to be angry

47

again. Lisa really didn't care as long as she could persuade her friend not to say something dreadful. It would be just like her to tell Rick she was crazy about him or something horrible like that.

When they got to Brewster Florist, Lisa looked around for Rick. Molly called out to them, "Hi, girls. Come on over here."

Lisa and Angela walked through the long, lovely display room that was jammed full of silk flowers and decorative plants in fancy holders of one kind or another. Lisa especially admired the wide pool in the center of the room. Several shelves that looked like rocks stood in the pool and each of them was packed with darling little arrangements.

There was a small fountain in the center of the pool and water sounds trickled down the rocks. Lisa loved the room and would have liked to stay there a long time. She'd been in Brewster Florist a couple of times before to buy gift plants for people in the hospital. But somehow, today, she was seeing things more clearly than she ever had before.

"I wonder what they feed the fish," Angela said. She was pointing to the large red and orange fish swimming around in the pool. "That's as big a goldfish as I've ever seen," she said.

"I'm not sure it is a goldfish," Lisa said. "We'll have to ask Molly."

"They sure do have a lot of flowers in here," Angela said with wonder in her voice. Again, Lisa felt a stab of fear. She dreaded what Angela might say or do. Why hadn't she been brave enough to come alone?

Molly looked red-faced and out of breath as she greeted Lisa. She said, "Welcome to the Palm Sunday open house. Things aren't going too well. My boss,

Rick's father, called early this morning to say he had to stay in Boston. His mother's brother is sick and he's the one who has to take care of things. Now Rick has disappeared. The other woman who's supposed to be helping has a sick kid. So, you see, things aren't quite the way they're supposed to be."

"It looks lovely," Lisa assured her. "Your bouquets of spring flowers are just wonderful." She turned to the work counter that was lined with small bouquets of carnations, pompoms, daffodils and statice.

"I wanted more varieties. Violets would have been nice. But they don't keep well. Neither do tulips."

"Aren't those tulips over there?" Angela asked.

"Yes," Molly said, "but they're potted plants." When she saw the look of bewilderment on Angela's face, she explained. "We sell lots of different things. Those flowers you saw in the front of the store are artificial—many of them are silk and made in other parts of the world. Then we se. plants that we grow in our greenhouses or buy from wholesalers. Cut flowers are a small part of our sales, but we do a lot of floral arrangements and, of course, we use cut flowers for those."

"Then what are the tulips—plants or flowers?" Angela asked.

"They're flowering bulbs," Molly said. "Besides tulips, we also have begonias that flower from something like a bulb. But it's called a tuber."

"Too much for me," Angela said. Then she walked away from Molly and Lisa and went over to the cash register. She laughed and said, "What a funny, old-fashioned cash register. How old is it?"

"It belonged to Mr. Brewster's father," Molly answered. "It might be about one hundred years old."

"Is that your real cash register?" Angela asked, pointing to a large, modern-looking machine that resembled the fancy cash registers in supermarkets.

"No, that's our Teleprompter computer," Molly said. "Orders for flowers come from all over the world onto that machine. For instance, this morning, I took an order for a dozen roses for Mrs. Whitaker on Fenn Street. The flowers were bought and paid for by her son Ronald, who lives in San Dimas, California."

"How much do a dozen roses cost?" Angela asked.

"It depends on the time of year. Today, they cost thirty-five dollars, plus tax and a two-dollar delivery charge; that makes it close to forty dollars."

Lisa was getting worried about all the questions that Angela was asking. Most of them seemed harmless enough, but Lisa knew her friend. Somehow, she would get around to saying or doing something to try and help Lisa with her interest in Rick. Lisa tried to stem the flow of questions by saying, "Molly, you go ahead and do whatever you have to do; we'll just look around."

"I'm through, at least for the moment. Since you're the only two in here, I'm happy to answer your questions. After all, Lisa, you were my star student."

That's when it happened. Angela blurted out, "Why don't you give Lisa a job here? She likes flowers."

Lisa's face flushed and her hands began to sweat. She wanted to turn and yell at her friend, but she didn't dare as long as Molly was standing there.

Molly looked rather startled by Angela's question and she answered, "We don't really need any help. But it's an idea for the future."

Just then another group of people came into the florist shop and Molly said, "I'll leave you now to look around on your own. Help yourself to the cider and cookies."

The minute Molly was out of hearing distance, Lisa turned to Angela and said in a fierce whisper, "How could you? I asked you especially not to say anything dumb. Honestly, Angela, I think you do it on purpose. Why did you?"

Lisa's eyes were smarting from tears she was holding back. She knew her face was flushed with anger and she was glad that Rick was not around for the open house. It would kill her to have him see her looking so angry. But she was angry—so angry that she wanted to reach out and shake Angela.

Angela's face changed from surprise to anger of her own. She said in a loud voice, "I don't know what you're so excited about. You act as though the whole world should be the way you want it. Who cares if you're silly about Rick Brewster. He doesn't care a thing about you and he never will!" With that, Angela turned and left the florist shop.

Lisa looked at her friend's departing back. She was still very angry, but now she was experiencing a different kind of bad feeling at the same time. She was pretty sure that this quarrel with Angela was more serious than the old quarrels. For a long time they'd been growing apart, and she was afraid that this was the end of a friendship. The sick feeling she had in her stomach was the feeling of loss.

Lisa was getting ready to go home herself, waiting only for Angela to have time to get far ahead of her. But before she could leave, Molly called to her. "Lisa, could you help me?"

Lisa turned and saw Molly struggling to balance two flowerpots in her hands while she held a box of lilies against the wall with her knee. It looked as though Molly were close to a big accident. Lisa ran over to her, taking the flowerpots from her hands so that Molly could push the box of lilies back onto the shelf without letting them tip over.

Molly turned to Lisa and said, "Thanks. It was dumb, but I was in such hurry that I messed up."

Lisa bent over the box of lilies and straightened a couple of the pots. She said, "Where do you want these?"

Molly was carrying two toward some customers in the front of the store. She turned her head and said, "Put them on the shelf by the cash register. We've sold out."

Carefully, so their stalks wouldn't get tangled, Lisa separated the lilies from each other and carried them to the empty shelf by the cash register. When she was finished, she picked up the empty cardboard box and carried it to the back room where she'd seen some others stacked. Then she brushed the heavy black dirt off her hands and went back to the center of the store.

Molly was at the cash register, ringing up the sale of lilies. She called to Lisa, "Will you bring me a small box from the back room?"

Lisa turned obediently and walked toward the back room, returning with a small cardboard box that she thought would fit the two lilies that Molly was selling.

After that, Molly asked her to get some string down from the tallest shelf. Then she helped Molly carry a large potted palm out to a man's car. As they huffed and puffed Molly said, "Darn that kid. He should be back by now."

"Where is he?" Lisa asked.

"Delivering plants. But he said he'd be back before

the shop opened. He's not here and neither is his father. Sometimes I think the Brewsters think I'm a steam truck instead of a five-foot-three woman."

As Molly grumbled she worked as quickly and efficiently as anyone Lisa had ever seen. She bent to the floor, then climbed to the tallest shelf, then smiled and chatted with customers, all at the same time it seemed to Lisa. Lisa followed Molly around, helping her whenever she could and sometimes anticipating her needs.

By the time Rick arrived at one o'clock, Lisa's white trousers were covered with mud and dirt. Her carefully combed hair was falling in her face and she was sure her makeup was mixed with a generous amount of mud. Instead of being embarrassed, she asked, "Where were you? Molly was worried about you."

"Looks like Molly had help," Rick said as he grinned. "I had four flat tires. Some clown let all the air out of my tires out on Barker Road. I'd like to kill the kid, but I couldn't catch him." He paused and smiled at Lisa again. "Anyway, thanks for doing my work."

Lisa left the Brewster flower shop at five that afternoon. She was covered with dirt and tired, but as happy as she'd been in years. For one thing, Rick gave her a ride home. For another thing, he actually seemed interested in her, asking her about herself, her family and hobbies.

As they sat in front of her house Rick held his hands lightly on the steering wheel of the truck and told her again how much he appreciated her help that day. "It was really good of you, Lisa. You're a good kid."

Lisa slid out of the truck and floated up to the front door, as though she were Cinderella on her way to the ball. She was so dazzled by Rick's charm that she almost didn't see John sitting on a chair inside her living room. When she did see him, she said, "Oh, John, I'm so sorry. I forgot all about our date."

John's face fell and he asked shyly, "Do you want to cancel?"

Lisa felt a rush of shame. "No, of course not. I'll be ready in about fifteen minutes. It will take me a minute to shower, and then we'll go. Will we be too late?"

John's face brightened and he shook his head. "No. It's an outdoor concert. One of those kinds that go on and on. We won't miss much."

Lisa ran from the room, feeling wonderful about her great day with Rick. She was even glad to be going out with John this evening. It would be fun to hear folk music.

5

The next week at school, Rick seemed even friendlier than before. He often stopped to talk with her in art class and Lisa began to hope that he might be a little interested in her. She knew there was nothing in his manner to make her feel that way, but she still hoped.

Still, he never invited her to work at his table. Nor did he ever stop to talk long when she met him in the cafeteria or the hallway. It was always a friendly grin and a fast hello but nothing more. Much as she wanted to believe, she couldn't help but notice that his manner was very different with her than it was with Patty Baker, for instance.

Once, she turned a corner and saw Rick talking to Patty beside the girl's locker. Rick was leaning on the locker door, his arm above his head. His body was tilted slightly down, as though he wanted to hear every word that Patty was saying. Patty was looking up at him, smiling happily. Her laughter tinkled in Lisa's ears as she walked past the happy couple.

Lisa felt tall, stiff and awkward as she passed them and did not speak to Rick. Only when he called out to her, "Hey, Lisa, hi," did she turn and smile at him.

She was sure it was hopeless, and yet she kept hoping. Each night Lisa stared at the telephone, willing it to ring. She didn't even want to admit to herself how much she hoped that by some magical happening Rick would decide to invite her to the prom.

The prom was three weeks away and a lot of the girls were already talking about what they would wear and whom they would go with. Lisa was pretty sure that John Reesner was going to ask her but she hadn't decided whether or not she would go. Did she really want to go to the prom with anyone but Rick?

Dating John was getting to be a habit, and a rather nice one at that. After that first date when they'd run out of conversation, matters got easier between them. Lisa noticed that John usually asked her to do things that they might both enjoy and that didn't require a lot of talking. John was a nice boy, but he wasn't much of a talker. Since Lisa tended to be quiet herself, it was good when they didn't have to try hard to find something to say. They were going bicycling that Saturday afternoon, and that would be fun.

John, who liked outdoor activities, had suggested the date. He'd looked rather scared as he waited for Lisa to make up her mind. One of the things that bothered Lisa about John was the way he always acted half scared of her. She knew that John had the same sort of crush on her that she had on Rick, and it made her very uncomfortable. Lisa sighed and thought, Why don't things ever work out right?

Her father looked up from his paper and asked, "What's that big sigh for?"

"She's in love," Eddie answered promptly.

"Eddie, I warned you," her mother put in.

Lisa said crossly, "I can't even breathe without everyone getting into a fight about it. Why don't you all mind your own business?"

"Lisa!" Her mother's voice was genuinely shocked.

"I'm sorry," Lisa said. "But it is true that you all seem to be watching me all the time. It makes me nervous."

"You are our business," her father said in a joking voice. "As for watching you, I don't see how you even noticed. You seem to spend all your time watching the telephone. Are you expecting a message?"

Knowing that her reaction was way out of proportion to the conversation, Lisa fought back tears. But she couldn't keep the tightness out of her throat as she said, "I just have the feeling that you're all waiting for me to do something. That you're all watching me."

"We're watching you watch the telephone, and now it appears that you're watching us watch you watch the telephone," her father said.

Lisa knew he was trying to help but she didn't care. She said, "I think I'll go to bed."

"It's only seven; are you sick?" her mother asked.

"That's what I mean," Lisa accused. She was really close to tears now, but she knew she would only upset everyone more if she gave in to them.

Her mother sighed and said, "You're so sensitive, Lisa. I'll be glad when you grow out of this phase. Whatever it is."

Lisa didn't answer. She picked up her magazine and went upstairs to her own room. As she closed the door behind her, she wished that she had a telephone of her own. Other girls did. But then, some girls didn't even have rooms of their own. She thought of her friend Angela, who had to share her bedroom with her ten-year-old sister. Everything that Angela did was reported to the family immediately. Lisa smiled as she remembered the time Angela was trying to turn her hair red by light applications of henna. She'd thought that if she did it in stages her family wouldn't notice. Of course, her little sister told on her and that was the end of the red hair.

Thinking of Angela made her feel sad again. She threw herself on her bed and stared up at the ceiling, letting the tears she'd been fighting all evening come rolling down her face. Nothing seemed to be going right in her life. Angela was still angry at her about the scene in the flower shop. Twice Lisa had tried to make up and both times Angela had been cool and distant.

Without Angela, she really didn't have any good friends at school. Girlfriends were important, too, and yet she didn't know anyone she wanted to know better. That led her to think about Patty Baker. Patty always had lots of friends, both male and female. Somehow, the thought of Patty's small blond cheerfulness was too much for Lisa. The quiet tears became heavy sobs.

Lisa buried her face in the pillow and sobbed and sobbed. As she cried, she thought about all the things she wanted that she didn't have. She wanted to be five feet five inches tall and blond. She wanted to be quick and cool when she talked to people. She wanted to be smarter, prettier and more perfect. She wanted . . . she wanted Rick Brewster to love her. That was what she wanted more than anything in the world, and she was never, never going to get that. No, Rick would never be anything more than friendly to a girl like her—a girl with long legs and straight black hair. A girl who couldn't seem to do anything at all but sigh and feel sorry for herself.

As she sobbed, her brother Eddie came to her door and called, "Telephone."

Lisa said, "I can't answer. Take a message."

Eddie didn't call back and Lisa assumed it was Angela or John on the telephone. At that moment, the last thing in the world she wanted to do was talk to either of them. She knew they would think she was crazy if she tried to tell them how she was feeling. For that matter, she knew her folks would think she was crazy too. But Lisa didn't care. In a way, it felt good to finally be sobbing and letting all the old, horrible thoughts out.

Lisa cried until she could cry no more. Then she put on her pajamas and got into bed. She went to sleep quickly and slept well. It was six thirty when she woke again.

Pulling on her robe, she went to the bathroom and brushed her teeth fiercely, to erase the grim taste in her mouth. She remembered that she'd forgotten to brush them the night before. She also remembered the desperate sadness that she had felt. But those thoughts seemed to belong to the forgotten past. Her mood had completely changed, and Lisa felt like whistling as she descended the stairs and went into the kitchen.

She was the first one up, so she put on the water for coffee and opened a can of frozen orange juice, mixing it with water in the blender. Then she made herself some toast and sat at the kitchen table, eating marmalade and toast and looking out the window at two brown birds who were perched on a limb close to the window. It was spring now, Lisa thought, and there were a lot of birds around. She knew that John was a good birder. Maybe she would get him to teach her about birds when she went out with him on Saturday.

Her good mood held all the way through breakfast. At one point, she laughed loudly at one of her father's silly jokes. He seemed pleased and repeated it. The second time, she laughed louder. He said, "You'll make someone very happy with that laugh one day. Especially if you marry a joker."

"Any man who married her would be a joker," Eddie said promptly.

Instead of getting mad, Lisa pulled Eddie's baseball cap down over his eyes and said, "You can be the flower boy at my wedding."

"Flowers . . ." Eddie said. "That phone call was from a flower shop."

"Brewster's Florist?" Lisa asked incredulously.

Eddie nodded, jamming too much toast into his mouth. "Said he'd call back tonight."

"It was a man? Was it . . . was it Rick Brewster?"

Eddie shrugged.

"Didn't you ask? I told you to get a message!" Lisa realized that she was shouting now.

Eddie looked at her for a moment, then said, "Boy, you're too much. One minute you're happy and the next minute you're screaming. I don't know who it was. Brewster flower shop, that's all I know."

Lisa fought hard to control herself. She knew it was her own fault that she'd been so upset she couldn't talk. She said, as calmly as she could, "I'll just have to wait and see, won't I?"

But despite her attempts at calmness, she couldn't

help feeling a little excited all morning as she waited for
art class. Her reason told her that if Rick had made a
personal phone call, he would have left his name, not
the name of the shop. Still, she hoped and hoped.
Maybe it really was Rick and maybe he really was going
to ask her to the prom. Maybe.

6

She was nervous when she walked into art class but she tried hard not to show it. Rick, who took two art classes in a row, was working hard on his painting and did not look up as she said, "Hi, Rick."

"Hi, Lisa. How's tricks?"

"Did you call me last night?" Lisa asked. She felt her voice was more of a whisper than a normal speaking voice.

Rick looked up then, with a perplexed frown on his face. "No, I was out all evening with Patty," he said. "We went to the movies. Why? Did you think I called?"

Lisa felt her face flush with shame and disappointment. But for once she managed to keep her voice steady as she said, "My little brother took a message. He said it was some flower shop. I thought it might be you."

Rick shook his head. Then he said, "I wonder if Molly called you."

"My brother said it was a man. Why would Molly call?"

Rick looked sorry he'd said anything and quickly went back to his work. Lisa turned and went to her table, wishing she hadn't said anything at all. Rick would think she was foolish, wondering if he'd called her. Still, Rick didn't seem to act as though he thought it was too strange. Lisa sighed and picked up the roll of wire she was going to use for her final project of the year.

As a first-year student, she had to spend the last six weeks of school on one project. Ms. Martino had given them several choices of media, and Lisa had chosen to do a wire and paper sculpture. As she'd envisioned the project, it would be large and impressive. She was actually hoping that it would be good enough that she could use it in her room.

Now she looked at her preliminary sketches and wondered if she'd ever even be able to get the framework to resemble what she'd put on the paper. Working with wire was strenuous, tough work, and her hands hurt by the time she'd put in ten minutes. Even so, Lisa kept right on working, and by the end of the period she was still huffing and puffing over the first part of the tree trunk.

"You want some help with that?" Rick's voice asked behind her.

Lisa straightened up and put her hands on her hips, stretching her back for a moment to relieve the tense muscles. "No, thanks," she said. "I'm determined to do it by myself. I'm going to get this darn thing right—or else."

"What is it?" Rick teased. He had been in the group when she'd presented her plans to the class, explaining carefully that she had in mind a wire and paper representation of a small clump of trees in the forest. The work was to be about two and a half feet high and two feet square.

"It's my enchanted forest," Lisa said. "Or at least I hope it will be. I am afraid I'll mess the whole thing up or, worse yet, I'll never learn how to bend wire well enough to make the tree trunks."

"Oh, you'll learn," Rick said. "You know, for a slender person, you're really very strong."

Before Lisa could think of anything to say to that, Patty Baker called from the doorway, "Hey, you two, the bell rang."

As Rick joined Patty, Lisa turned to put her sculpture parts away. She would be late to history class, but it was worth it. She'd had a long conversation with Rick, and that was worth a great deal.

But that night, as she sat in her living room staring at the telephone, she kept thinking about the way Rick had called her strong. She didn't mind it if he thought she was strong as much as she minded the fact that he'd called her skinny. Well, he hadn't really called her skinny, but slender and skinny were almost the same thing, weren't they?

The telephone did ring while she was looking at it. In fact, it rang three times. The first call was from John, who asked her if she would like to go to the prom with him. Lisa opened her mouth to say yes, but the words wouldn't come out. She said, "John, can I tell you later? I'll have to check with my mother."

"Look, Lisa, if you don't want to, you don't have to go with me," John said. "I understand."

"It's not that," Lisa lied. "It's just that I have to check it out with my mother. Sometimes she has funny ideas about things; you know how mothers are."

When she put the telephone down, her mother looked at her with a quizzical raise of the eyebrow but didn't ask any questions. Lisa was grateful for that. She knew her mother disapproved of lying, and she felt guilty about it herself. She knew she would probably go to the prom with John, but she just had to give herself time for the miracle to happen. Miracles did happen, didn't they? Patty could break a leg or something.

Frowning in shock at her own thoughts, Lisa jumped when the telephone rang again. Letting it ring twice, she picked up the receiver and said hello. This time it was Angela, who wanted some help on the history homework.

They talked for a while, and Lisa was glad that Angela had actually called her. Though the two girls were friends again, Lisa noticed that Angela was much more reserved and careful about how she behaved around Lisa. In a way, Lisa missed the old Angela who never gave a thought to anything she said. This new, removed Angela made Lisa feel unsure of what to say or do herself.

After they'd finished the homework, Angela asked, "Are you going to the prom with John?"

"I'm not sure," Lisa said. "He asked me, but . . ."

"But you're hoping that Rick will call you."

Was that disapproval in Angela's voice? Lisa couldn't be sure, but she didn't feel like taking a chance. She repeated the same lie. "I have to check with my mother. I explained that to John."

"Sure, Lisa," Angela said. They talked for a few more minutes and then hung up.

As Lisa turned back to her magazine she wondered about the now obvious disapproval in Angela's voice. Why did Angela care whether or not she kept John waiting? After all, it was three weeks until the night of the prom, so she had a right to let herself hope a little.

When the telephone rang a third time, Lisa made no move to get it. Her father said, "Pick it up, Lisa. All the calls are for you these days."

Rather than argue with her father, Lisa started toward the telephone, but this time Eddie beat her to it. He listened for a minute and then said, "Lisa, it's that same guy."

When Lisa took the telephone this time, her hands were shaking. So was her voice as she said hello.

A man's voice said, "Good, you're there. This is Adam Brewster of Brewster Florist. I told my manager, Molly, that I'd call you and talk to you about a Saturday morning job. You'd be helping Molly in the shop on Saturday mornings while I play golf." He stopped for a soft chuckle and continued. "I believe you know Molly and my son Rick. They say you're a good worker and they'll let me off the leash if I hire you as a replacement. How about it?"

"What?" Lisa said. Her mind was whirling as she tried to understand what Mr. Brewster was saying.

"I want you to work on Saturday mornings, from eight till noon. I'll pay you minimum wage. Will you do it?"

"Yes."

"Good, that's settled. See you Saturday morning. No, I'm wrong. I won't see you. Molly and Rick will see you. I'll be golfing." He laughed again and hung up.

As Lisa replaced the telephone she thought about Rick's father and the way he laughed at his own jokes.

She wondered if he was a friend of her father's. They both talked that same way, with every other sentence laced with some small joke. Then she wondered if it bothered Rick the way it bothered her to have a father who made jokes all the time.

This time, her mother couldn't keep from asking questions. "Who was that? And what did he want?"

"That was the man who owns Brewster Florist. He gave me a job on Saturday mornings." Lisa answered. She was beginning to understand how wonderful that job might be. After all, she would be working with Rick all the time, wouldn't she?

"You told him you would work?" her mother asked.

"Yes. Is that all right?" Lisa knew that her mother always liked her to help with the housework on Saturday morning. Since her parents worked all week and she was in school, a lot of things had to be accomplished on Saturdays.

"I suppose it is all right," her mother said. "I just find it interesting that you feel free to accept a job without consulting your father and me. And at the same time you tell that poor boy that you can't go to the dance until we approve." She looked at her daughter with an expression that seemed to be halfway between displeasure and amusement. "We approve of John, you know. He's a nice fellow."

Lisa felt funny to have her mother so obviously aware of what she'd done about John. She felt she owed her mother some explanation, but she hated to admit the truth. Finally, she did say, "There's another fellow I'm hoping will ask me. I know he won't, but I hope he will. Oh, you wouldn't understand."

Her mother smiled then and said, "I might. But it really isn't fair to John to keep him waiting long.

Promise me you'll give him an answer early next week. He'll need time to invite another girl when your dreamboat calls you."

"He won't," Lisa said sadly. Then she looked at her mother with a new interest and asked, "Dreamboat? Did you really use that word when you were young?"

"There he is, my dreamboat," her mother said.

Sam Kelly smiled and added, "Your mother was the most popular girl in our class."

"That's not quite the truth," her mother protested. "But it's nice that he remembers it that way."

Lisa told herself that it probably was close to the truth. Her mother was a beautiful woman, and only five feet six inches tall. Her mother and Eddie looked a lot alike.

But Lisa knew her mother was right about stalling John too long. She promised herself that she would give Rick a chance to ask her to the prom on the Saturday morning of her first day at work. After that, she would tell John she accepted his invitation. She just couldn't give up on the possibility that Rick might ask her until she saw him one time at work. After all, he'd told his father he knew her. Perhaps he'd also recommended her for the job. If only he'd wanted her to work there because he was interested in her. Then it would be her dream come true. If only . . .

But Lisa's hopes were quickly dimmed on Saturday morning when she went to work at Brewster Florist. In the first place, she found out that Rick spent most of his time driving the delivery truck. He was in and out of the shop, but most of the time he was in a rush to get the next plant or bouquet to the next customer. Beyond a friendly hello and good wishes, Lisa didn't exchange three words with him. It was Patty Baker who told her that Rick was taking her to the dance.

Patty came in about eleven o'clock, looking sweet and cool in a yellow print shirt and white shorts. When she saw Lisa, who was sweating as she moved some pots of geraniums from the potting shed to the front display area, Patty wasn't surprised. She said, "Hi, Lisa. Rick told me you were going to work here. How do you like it?"

Lisa brushed the hair away from her face and answered, "I like it fine." She didn't tell Patty that, so far, all she'd done was lug heavy plants around and water some of the bedding flats.

"That's good," Patty said. "I think you'll be good for the job, you're so tall. And Rick says you're strong."

Lisa flushed and didn't answer. Patty went on, "I just came by to tell Rick that I've bought a yellow dress for the prom. What color is yours?"

"I don't know." Lisa's heart was sinking in disappointment. Though she'd expected it all along, she'd hoped . . . but she didn't dare let Patty see that disappointment. Patty would think she was foolish to believe that Rick could be even slightly interested in her. She said, "I haven't picked out my dress yet."

"Well, you'd better get one early," Patty warned. "They're going to be picked over very quickly. Of course, you probably wear a bigger size, but the size fives were almost gone."

"I wear a twelve," Lisa said. The way Patty talked, you'd think she was a monster or something.

"Anyway, will you tell Rick my dress is yellow? I want him to start thinking of the sort of flowers I'm going to wear." She smiled and added, "Rick always

69

brings me a lovely corsage. I think it's good advertising."

Molly called Lisa to come and help her with something and Lisa said good-bye to Patty. She was glad to get away from the girl who seemed to have everything she'd ever wanted. Though she had to admit that Patty was friendly enough, she could never really like her. Lisa knew it was because she was too jealous of Patty to be comfortable around her. "You've got to get your act together," Lisa mumbled to herself as she struggled to move a large container for Molly.

Rick didn't come back to the shop before it was time for Lisa to leave, so she was spared the pain of relaying Patty's message about the flowers. She met Mr. Brewster, who came in from golf looking happy and tanned. He shook her hand and told her he hoped she'd be very happy working for them. "My son told me you were a big, strong girl. He didn't tell me you were beautiful. But I should have known," Mr. Brewster said.

Lisa knew it was only a joke but she was glad Mr. Brewster had called her beautiful, even if it wasn't true. She liked the man, she thought as she walked toward her home. It was easy to see where Rick got his easy good manners and his charm.

As she turned into her driveway she saw John sitting on the porch. He looked young and cute sitting in the sunlight, talking with Eddie. She called out, "Hi, John. I'll be ready in ten minutes. Did Eddie tell you I have a job?"

"Yes," John said.

She could tell just by looking at him that he was nervous again. Why was he acting that nervous about a simple little date to ride out in the country and look at nature? Then she knew that it was because he was

waiting for her answer about the prom. Poor Jo
was as bad as she was about wearing his heart on his
sleeve.

She smiled down at him and said, "I will be happy to
go to the prom with you."

"You will?" His face was a bright poster of happiness.

"Yes," Lisa said, "Yes, I will."

7

Lisa called Angela and asked her if she would like to go shopping with her. "We could look for dresses in the afternoon and then go to the movies. My folks will let me have the car all day Saturday."

"No, thanks," Angela said. "I won't be able to go."

"Aren't you going to the prom? I thought you'd decided to ask your cousin if you didn't have a date."

"I'm going to the prom, but I won't be able to go shopping."

"I could wait," Lisa offered. "Maybe I could get the car one evening next week."

"My mother and I are going to pick out my dress," Angela explained. Then she quickly changed the subject. "Did you study for the history exam tomorrow?"

Though Angela and she didn't have any of the same classes, they shared the same teacher for history. He usually gave each of the girls' classes the same tests.

Lisa and Angela talked for a few more minutes and then Lisa hung up the telephone. She felt sad that her friend seemed so removed and withdrawn these days. She didn't really understand why Angela remained angry about that day in the flower shop. Lisa had apologized more than once, and each time Angela insisted that she wasn't angry. Yet Lisa was certain that something was wrong. Angela was friendly but she never initiated any activities anymore. In fact, she usually turned Lisa down when she called and asked her to do something.

Lisa didn't want to go shopping alone, so she asked her mother if she would go with her. Her mother was pleased and seemed to enjoy the day in the shopping mall. They went from store to store, looking at prom dresses. Some of them were quite expensive and some were very beautiful, but they didn't find exactly the right thing.

Over a lunch of spinach quiche and watercress salad, Lisa said, "I think the green dress we saw in the first shop will do. It was pretty . . . and my feet are getting tired."

"So are mine," her mother admitted. "But we're not going to buy a dress that will just 'do.' This is a special night for a special girl, and we're going to find a dress that will be special." Her mother added, "Lisa, someday you'll recognize what a very individual beauty you have. Then you'll be happier. But in the meantime, you must find something that . . . that isn't . . ."

"That isn't made for pretty little girls?" Lisa finished her mother's sentence ruefully. "It's all right, Mother. I'm getting used to it." She made a face. "Molly and Mr. Brewster rave all the time about how wonderful it is that I'm so big and strong. They make me feel like Paul Bunyan or someone."

Her mother smiled and picked up the check. "I'm glad you're gaining some perspective. That job is good for you."

"I love the job," Lisa said. That was true. Though she'd taken it, in part, to be close to Rick, she'd loved it from the very first day. She loved the plants and flowers. She even enjoyed lifting boxes and doing the cleanup. The physical exercise felt good.

"Let's go to Reynold's," her mother suggested.

"But, Mother, that's sixty miles from here. Besides, it's very expensive."

"I'll call your father and tell him we'll be late. As for expense, there's one thing about being a woman who works: If I want to spend a fortune on a dress for my beautiful daughter, that's my business."

They drove from the shopping mall back through their town to another mall on the other side of the state. As she pulled into the parking lot of the second mall, Lisa said, "I think we're going to find the perfect one here."

"If we don't, we can always call and have the green dress mailed," her mother assured her. "But we'd better hurry. There's only an hour until closing time."

They didn't need an hour to find the perfect dress. As soon as they walked into the gown department of Reynold's, Lisa spied the most beautiful dress she'd ever seen, hanging on a rack. Her heart began beating rapidly as she pointed and said, "There it is. That's the dress."

Her mother said, "Let's check the size before you get too excited."

"But that's my dress," Lisa said. She was as excited

as she'd been when she was younger at Christmas time. She reached out and touched the beautiful soft chiffon skirt as her mother looked at the price tag and frowned.

"Is it too expensive?" Lisa whispered. Her mind began whirling with ways to make up the difference in money. If she turned all her paychecks over for the next two months . . .

"It's not the money, though it isn't cheap," her mother said. "But it is a size eight."

"Oh," Lisa said. She felt the tears coming to her eyes again. How embarrassing! She was getting to be the biggest crybaby in the world. Now she wanted to cry over a silly dance dress. You'd think it was her mind that was soft, not the beautiful fabric she held in her hand.

A small, dark salesperson came over to them and said energetically, "The dress is perfect for her, isn't it? Look at that color. Exactly the same as her eyes."

"We'd like to see the size twelves," Lisa said.

"The dress will fit you," the saleswoman promised. "That's why it is on sale. It ran very tall. Not big, but tall. It will fit you."

Lisa's heart began to beat in hope. If only that were true! Again, she ran her fingers over the soft blue-lavender dress. She said in a small voice, "I could try it on."

"Maybe we should look at some others first," her mother said doubtfully.

"Let's try the perfect dress first," the saleswoman said. "Then, if I am not right, we will look for others. But this dress is perfection. It is the color of blue skies at dawn, the color of robins' eggs in the spring, the color of the young woman's eyes. You are in love with the dress—yes?"

"Yes," Lisa whispered.

"Then true love must be served," the woman said briskly and hustled Lisa off to a dressing room.

Three minutes later, Lisa walked out onto the floor of Reynold's Department Store to show her mother the dress. Her mother's face looked surprised, then delighted as she said, "It really is perfect, isn't it?"

Lisa smiled and nodded her head. "It's a magic dress," she said. "I feel . . . I feel . . . beautiful."

The saleswoman and her mother laughed. "You are," they said in unison.

As the saleswoman took her mother's check and handed Lisa the box she rattled on about the wonderful things that would happen to Lisa in the dress. She promised joy, happiness and love ever after. Lisa stood smiling, half believing what the woman was saying. As they left the department the woman took her hand and whispered, "It will bring you love—you'll see. I am part Gypsy."

Lisa didn't really believe her, but she was entertained and happy because the woman had been so enthusiastic. Of course, she would have bought the dress, no matter what. Never in her life had she seen such a beautiful color.

On the night of the dance, she dressed early and went downstairs to pose for pictures. She'd made her folks promise not to take John's picture when he came to pick her up. That would have been too embarrassing. But she really didn't mind posing for the photographs herself. She wanted a record of how she felt and looked that night. She knew that she looked beautiful, and she couldn't help but be surprised that the dress made that much difference.

She looked at the Polaroid photos carefully, noting

her high, bright cheeks and her lavender-blue eyes that were exactly the color of the dress. Her long black hair was shining like velvet and her mouth turned up in a lovely smile. She looked at the photos for a long time, hoping to convince herself that the girl who looked back at her was really herself.

Finally, she said, "I'm hungry. I think I'll get a piece of cake."

"Lisa! You're not going to eat in that dress?"

"I'll be careful," Lisa promised, smiling. The funny thing was that she thought this evening meant as much to her mother as it did to her. Sue Kelly had spent the whole afternoon running in and out of Lisa's room, helping her get ready and giving her advice on how to handle the long, full skirt. She'd even offered Lisa her pearl necklace, but Lisa had preferred to wear the gown plain.

The soft Grecian folds across the front seemed enough without any adornment. Lisa was glad the dress had long sleeves, because she often felt as though her arms were too long in sleeveless blouses. Everything about this dress seemed to have been made for her, from the color to the length of the chiffon skirt.

As she leaned over the sink, eating cake and drinking milk, she had to admit that her attitude had something to do with how lovely she looked. She knew that her eyes and cheeks were sparkling more than usual. And certainly she was happy and smiling instead of feeling fearful and awkward. She poured herself a second glass of milk and wondered if she could look like this all the time if she were to smile more. Maybe it would help. Maybe she would try it. At any rate, she was certainly enjoying the way she felt today.

Her mother called, "Lisa, John is here."

Quickly Lisa brushed the crumbs from her mouth, rinsed the milk glass and straightened up. She held part of her skirt in one hand and prepared to glide into the living room. She knew that John, who was always so interested in her, would be impressed by the way she looked. She was going to enjoy the moment when she turned the corner. She felt a little like Cinderella on her way to the ball. Or even more like the Ugly Duckling turned into a swan, she thought.

John's reaction wasn't as great as she'd hoped. He smiled and said, "Hi, Lisa. I brought white flowers like you said." He held out a small corsage of white orchids.

Lisa looked down at the beautiful white flowers and wondered if they'd come from Brewster Florist. Perhaps Rick . . . but that was foolish. She had no business thinking about Rick now. This was her night—hers and John's—and she wasn't going to let anything spoil it. No sad thoughts and no shy wishes for something different. What was going on was good enough.

She said, "The flowers are lovely, John. I'll just pin them on." Then she turned and went to the hall mirror where she pinned the soft white flowers against the shoulder of her dress. Then, deciding that they might be crushed there, she moved them a little higher, so that they nestled on the side of the deep V neck of the dress, right beside her collarbone. Lisa smiled at her reflection. Funny how she'd always hated those collarbones that seemed to stick out every which way, just as she'd hated her long legs, long arms and high cheekbones. But tonight even her collarbones seemed perfect.

"You look like a model," John said as she came back into the living room. He was holding a photograph of her in his hand.

Ordinarily, Lisa would have been angry that her father had left the photos and camera in such a conspicuous spot. She knew Sam Kelly was obviously hoping she'd change her mind about having her photo taken with John. Did she really care more about being sophisticated than pleasing her father? Lisa asked herself.

"Dad, will you take a couple of photos of John and me?" she asked.

Her father's face brightened and he jumped right up. "Glad to," he answered.

For the next ten minutes, Lisa posed patiently with John as her father took shot after shot of them. They sat beside each other on the couch, then stood together by the fireplace. Next, Sam decided he wanted a shot of Lisa coming down the stairs with John standing below, looking up. For each shot, Lisa smiled patiently. In truth, she rather enjoyed looking at her newfound beauty in so many different poses. By the time her father was satisfied, Lisa was laughing at herself. Last week I wouldn't look in the mirror because I thought I was so homely. Now I can't stop looking because I think I'm so beautiful. It's the same face, but I've changed from a weepy wimp to a self-centered ninny. Ah, well! Lisa exclaimed to herself.

When her father asked them to pose getting into John's car, Lisa laughed out loud. "Absolutely not! You're spending a fortune on film, and John's car isn't a golden coach, you know."

"More like a pumpkin," John agreed quickly. "It's not exactly a scenic sight."

Nevertheless, her father followed them out to the little VW beetle and took a photo of Lisa stooping to get into the car. Lisa was laughing very hard by the time she had all her long, full skirts collected and tucked into the small auto. When John sat down beside her, she said, "You must forgive my father. He's very proud of me."

"He should be," John said quickly. Then he showed her the three photos that Sam Kelly had given him as keepsakes of the evening. His nice, open face was smiling and friendly as he said, "This is a night I'll always remember, Lisa. Thank you for coming with me."

Lisa flushed. She never knew what to say to John when he talked that way. She always felt uncomfortable with the knowledge that John was so much more interested in her than she was in him. She looked at him now, wondering if she could ever feel about him the way she felt about Rick Brewster. Sadly, she decided that it would never really be possible. John was a nice boy and she was having a very nice time with him, but John wasn't very exciting. It wasn't just that he wasn't good-looking. It was that he wasn't friendly or fun the way Rick was. When she was with John, she always felt she had to do the entertaining. With Rick, she could relax. Rick was so warm and friendly and happy-go-lucky that he was easy to be around.

But John was a nice person and Lisa did her very best to make sure that they both had a good time at the dance. She listened to him as he talked; she laughed at his small jokes. She didn't even blush when he showed the photos to a group of kids at the dance. When John asked her to dance, she got up quickly and followed him onto the floor.

Once a year Connors High School had a formal prom, and the student body always chose a dance band that played slow, quiet music. Though there were a few disco numbers, most of the music was soft and romantic. At first Lisa felt uncomfortable, trying to follow John, who seemed to stumble a lot. But later she got used to his simple dance steps and managed to keep up with him.

Though she tried very hard, Lisa couldn't help looking at the door every once in a while to see if Rick and Patty were coming in. A lot of kids thought it was smart to come to the dance very late. Some got all dressed up, came for one or two dances and then left, but Lisa couldn't believe that Rick would behave that way. Still, when Rick wasn't there by ten, Lisa was beginning to wonder where he was. Maybe Patty had gotten sick? Somehow, it was impossible to imagine Rick sick; he was too healthy.

At ten fifteen, Rick appeared in the doorway of the dance. Lisa's heart speeded up and she began to think hopefully that he might be alone. She excused herself from the table where they sat drinking Cokes and headed for the ladies' room. With just a little detour, she was able to get into Rick's view.

He saw her very quickly, and she was grateful for the look of admiration and surprise on his face as he greeted her. "Hi, Lisa. You look beautiful."

She moved closer to him, smiling happily, and said, "Thank you, Rick," and then she waited.

"Would you like to dance?" he asked.

She nodded yes and lifted her arms so that he could encircle her waist and lead her out onto the dance floor. They were playing a soft, dreamy song, and Lisa's body seemed to melt as she felt the firm pressure of Rick's hand on her back. Rick was a wonderful dancer and moved her through the room softly and easily. Because he was so good, Lisa felt easier with him than she had with John. She was able to keep her body loose and relaxed and dip and turn as easily as she'd hoped. After a while, she said, "You're a good dancer."

Rick laughed. "Before my mother died, we belonged to the country club. She made my brother and me go to dancing lessons every Thursday afternoon. I can do the tango, the waltz and the fox trot."

"What is this?" Lisa asked.

"This is . . . this is romantic dancing with a beautiful lady," Rick said. "Dreamy dancing," he added with a grin. "It has no other name."

"Dreamy dancing," Lisa repeated happily. She wondered if she dared move her head closer to his shoulder. They were exactly the same height and it would be easy enough to do. But the song ended before she had a chance to experiment with that bold plan.

Rick dropped his hand from her back but kept hold of her hand. He was smiling as he said, "Thanks, Lisa. You really do look beautiful tonight."

She smiled at him and at that moment she felt like the most beautiful woman in the world. If only the music had gone on and on forever. But life was not like that. Even good things had a time limit on them. And John was waiting for her. She said, "I was on my way to the ladies' room. Will I see you later?"

"I hope so," Rick answered smoothly. "Patty and I are planning to stay till the end. Maybe we can dance again."

"I hope so," Lisa answered, hoping also that the disappointment didn't show in her voice. So Patty was here—well, she hadn't really wanted Patty to break a leg. Or had she?

Lisa took her hand from Rick's and smiled at him

again. Then she went into the ladies' room as she'd planned.

When she came out, she saw Rick dancing with Patty. She tried not to look too carefully because she didn't want to spoil the wonderful feelings she had from dancing with him herself. As she walked back across the hall to John she could still feel the warmth of Rick's hand on the small of her back. Oh, if only . . .

"I'm sorry I'm late," Lisa said quickly. "I ran into Rick and danced with him."

"Yes, I saw," John said.

Lisa could hear the sadness in John's voice and promised herself that she would not dance with Rick again, even if he asked her. After all, it was John who had invited her to the dance. John was her date. And John was the one who was always so nice to her. He deserved better than to be made jealous on this night.

But Lisa didn't really have to make that promise to herself, because Rick didn't get around to asking her to dance again. Each time she looked out on the floor, she saw Patty and Rick twirling and dipping to the music. As the evening wore on, Lisa had to admit that Rick and Patty seemed to be having a good time.

Once, she saw them laughing together about something and she felt that old, sharp stab of jealousy. It was then that she allowed herself to really look at Patty Baker. The girl was beautiful, there was no doubt about that. Her yellow dress seemed to shimmer and glow in the colored lights of the dance hall. Patty was wearing her curly blond hair piled high on her head, and from her ears hung shining stones. Could they be real diamonds? Lisa wondered for a moment. She knew that Patty's folks were wealthy, but surely no teenage

girl would be allowed to wear diamond earrings to a
school dance?

But, diamonds or rhinestones, Patty looked lovely.
She wore a very large, dramatic corsage of purple iris
and lavender orchids. Lisa knew that they were so
special because Rick worked at Brewster's, but she
couldn't help comparing them to her own flowers.
Funny how the white orchids she wore had seemed so
wonderful three hours ago. Now they seemed ordinary.
She looked down at the skirt of her beautiful blue
chiffon dress. Was it ordinary, too?

"Are you tired?" John asked.

"Not really," Lisa said quickly and forced herself to
smile. Apparently John had picked up on her depressed
mood. That wouldn't do at all. She'd promised herself
that she and John would have a great time—no matter
what.

Well, they *were* having a great time and there hadn't
been any *no matter whats*. She and John were getting
along well. The kids they were with were all great.
She'd danced with Rick and he'd said she was beautiful.
It was an absolutely marvelous evening.

John kissed her when he brought her home. It was a
light, tentative kiss, and Lisa felt a little silly as she
slipped her arms around his neck and lifted her face to
his. As she kissed John she wondered what kissing Rick
would be like. Would it be even more awkward? After
all, John was several inches taller than she, so that
should make it easier. Yet Lisa was sure that kissing
Rick would be a lot different from this.

"Good night," she whispered. "I had a wonderful
evening."

"I'll call you tomorrow," John said. He looked very
happy standing under the porch light. Lisa was happy

too, but she knew that her happiness was more because of feeling that she'd looked beautiful than because of John. She wondered if it was fair to John to keep dating him when she really wasn't interested in him. But that was nothing to think about tonight. Tonight she would think only good things.

She wasn't really surprised to find her mother waiting up for her when she went into the house. Instead of making excuses, her mother grinned and asked, "Did you have fun? I was so hoping you would."

Lisa hugged her mother tightly and said, "I had a wonderful time! Oh Mother, it was so wonderful—I wish you could have been there. I danced with a lot of boys and every one of them told me I looked beautiful. Every one! John was nice and we both had fun. Thanks for the dress. The dress was magic."

"No, Lisa, you're the magic. Not the dress." Her mother yawned and asked, "Want some cake?"

"No, thanks. John and I went out for hamburgers with two other couples. That was fun too. I felt like a character in an old movie, sitting there in this wonderful dress, pouring more ketchup on my hamburger."

"Did Angela go with you?"

Lisa frowned. For the first time, she realized that she hadn't seen Angela at the dance at all. "No, we went with Mike and Ann and John and Sally," Lisa said. Then she added, "Mother, you know the boy I wanted to ask me, the the one I was hoping and waiting for . . ."

"The Brewster boy?"

"How did you know who he was?" Lisa asked.

Sue Kelly smiled. She answered, "Mothers know things. For instance, would you dress so carefully for that flower-shop job if you weren't interested in him?"

"Anyway," Lisa said quickly, "I danced with Rick and he said I was beautiful. I could tell he meant it. I saw it in his eyes." She rose and went softly, quickly, to her room. She wanted to go to sleep quickly and to dream of this wonderful night. And she wanted to dream of the future. A future that might include Rick Brewster. It might, Lisa told herself. Anyway, a girl has a right to dream.

8

After that magical prom night, the school year seemed to pass in a blur of activity and changes. Lisa and John spent a lot of time together, and that made up, in part, for the fact that Angela was barely speaking to her. Twice she tried to get her old friend to talk about the way they were growing apart. Both times Angela denied that there was a problem. Yet Lisa knew there was, and eventually she stopped calling Angela or trying to include her in activities.

John was just as faithful as ever and Lisa went out with him more and more often, though her feelings did not change. After that night, John had tried to kiss her again, but Lisa had drawn away gently. "I don't want to be serious," she'd explained. "In fact, I think we should both start dating other people."

"Of course," John said. "I never expected you not to

date other people. You're too beautiful and popular not to have other boyfriends."

Lisa smiled at him. It was hard not to be pleased when John called her beautiful, but she never knew exactly how to handle his obvious admiration. Sometimes she felt so exasperated with his dogged faithfulness that she was mean to him. This was one of those days. "I'm not talking about me. I'm talking about you. I want you to date other girls."

"But I don't want to," John said. His voice sounded a little like Eddie's when her younger brother wanted to stay up late at night.

"I'm not going out with you again until you've dated two other girls," Lisa pronounced.

Poor John called her two days later and proudly announced he had dates with Angela on Thursday and Sally on Friday. "Will you go out with me on Saturday night?" John asked.

Lisa groaned inwardly and then said yes. She really didn't know what she felt about John anymore. Sometimes she wondered if she liked him at all. Other times she wondered if she would like him a lot if it weren't for Rick Brewster. Still other times she just felt he was a nuisance and she wished he would go away. Yet she knew that John was making her feel better about herself. Having someone who was crazy about her was nice, even if she didn't return the feeling. John's love for her made her feel like an attractive and pretty girl. She knew it was helping her to have more confidence and be less shy.

That Saturday night, she and John ran into Rick and Patty after the movies. Rick was, as always, very friendly, and this night he suggested, "Let's all go get a hamburger together."

Immediately, Lisa's heart began to beat in anticipation. She knew that Rick was getting to like her better all the time. At work he was more and more friendly, and at school he spent a lot of time talking to her. True, he never dated anyone but Patty; but who knew what he would do in the future? There is a chance, Lisa promised herself. She tried to keep the excitement out of her voice as she said, "I think that would be great."

"But you said you have to go home early," John protested.

Again, Lisa felt anger at the whine in his voice. There were just too many times when John sounded like a little kid who didn't get his own way. Lisa was beginning to understand that John was not weak but, in his own fashion, managed to get what he wanted a lot of the time. He had her, didn't he?

Before she had a chance to say anything, Patty said she was tired and wanted to go home early. Rick looked at Lisa and grinned. "Looks like we're the only two with energy," he said.

"It's Lisa who's tired," John said quickly. "I'm only thinking of her."

Lisa smiled and shrugged her shoulders, hoping to express her helpless disappointment to Rick. That evening, she refused to let John kiss her good night. When he asked if she wanted to go swimming at the lake the next day, she said, "No. I'll be too tired." Then she went inside.

If Rick was disappointed that they hadn't gone out for a hamburger together, he didn't say so. On Monday, at school, Lisa said, "Sorry we couldn't go with you guys Saturday. Maybe some other time?"

"Sure," Rick said. "Now let me show you my final project. It's finished."

Lisa followed Rick over to the other side of the room and looked at his large oil painting which stood on an easel. "Oh, Rick," she breathed softly. "It's wonderful."

The painting was a portrait of a blond woman, but it was not an ordinary portrait at all. The woman's face was almost totally merged with the flower still life that was also there. The effect was of a transparent still life underneath which shimmered a golden woman. Lisa had seen it as it progressed, but this was the first time she'd seen it since Rick took it home a week ago to glaze it and put the final touches on it.

They stood side by side for quite a while. Lisa opened her mouth to tell him again how much she loved it, but she could find no words. Finally, she asked, "Who is the woman?"

"My dream girl," Rick said with a laughing voice.

"Patty?" she asked.

He looked startled at the suggestion. "No. It isn't anyone. It's just a face I dreamed one night. I dreamed all the flowers too." He waited a long while before he added, "I think it might be my mother. That is, I think, in the dream, it might have been my mother, but she didn't look like this."

"It's a wonderful painting," Lisa said. "You should be very proud."

"I am," Rick said. "How's the enchanted forest coming?"

Lisa groaned. "Horrible. It looks like nothing but gnomes and goblins could possibly live there. I'm so disappointed. I guess I bit off more than I could chew."

"No sense trying to chew wire," Rick teased. "Use pliers instead."

Lisa laughed loudly. Some other kids came over to

Rick's table to view the painting, and Lisa went back to her own work space feeling very good. Rick had sought her out specially to show her the painting. That meant something, didn't it? At least it meant that he counted her as a friend.

But if Lisa had expected more than friendship, she was disappointed. Rick's attitude remained constant during the last weeks of school. He continued to date Patty and speak to Lisa at school. Nevertheless, Lisa was pleased that they seemed to have more and more to say to each other. She was also happy to notice that she wasn't as nervous with him as she used to be.

It was Rick who told her about the summer job coming up at Brewster Florist. He said, "I know my dad thinks you're too young, but why don't you apply anyway? You could handle it."

Determined not to let a chance to be with Rick all day go by without a struggle, Lisa tackled Molly the next Saturday morning. She said, "Rick says you're going to be hiring someone for the summer months."

"A man. An older man," Molly said shortly. She was busy moving small geranium plants into two-inch pots.

"I'm sure I could do the work," Lisa said. "I'd like to try."

Molly stopped her work for a moment, rubbed her muddy hands on her Levi's and said, "I think you could, too. But I'm not the boss. The boss thinks you're too young." Then she made a face and added, "And too female. He keeps saying he wants a man to help me."

"But I'm strong," Lisa protested.

"Talk to Adam Brewster, don't talk to me."

That morning, Lisa worked especially hard, moving flats of plants, lifting large pots and doing anything and everything she could to be useful. When Mr. Brewster came in from his golf game at one, Lisa was ready for him. She said, "Mr. Brewster, I want to talk to you."

"Sure, kiddo. Come into my office." He smiled at Lisa, and she was reminded of his handsome son. Mr. Brewster was shorter and fatter than Rick and not nearly as good-looking, but he had that same wonderful smile.

Lisa followed him into the small, crowded work space that Mr. Brewster kept as his office. He took a stack of gardening magazines off the second chair and pointed for Lisa to sit down. She did so, saying, "I want to apply for the summer job you have open."

He frowned and said, "Who told you there was a summer job? Never mind; that darn kid of mine told you. The job is taken. I'm sorry."

"I'm a good worker," Lisa said quickly. "I can lift things. I haven't made any big mistakes." She thought briefly of the day she'd drowned a whole flat of succulents but decided that was only a little mistake. "Molly says she's satisfied with my work. I like it here."

He was shaking his head, lighting a cigar and frowning at the wall. "Sorry, kiddo. The job is taken."

Lisa wondered if that was really true or if he was just saying that to make it easier to turn her down. She was feeling silly for pursuing the matter, but at the same time she really wanted the job. "Won't you at least tell me why I wasn't considered for the job?" she asked.

"Too young," he said briefly. "Lisa, I'm sorry, but you're just not the person I had in mind for the job. I want someone to take some of the load off Molly's back. Someone who can help her more."

"I can help her," Lisa answered quickly. At least she

had him talking now. At least she wasn't just getting a flat no. "Ask Molly if I'm not a big help to her. I can lift things—I'm strong. I'm easy to work with. I'm helpful. I'll bet, if she'd show me, I could even do simple flower arrangements for her."

Mr. Brewster seemed to be considering the idea. Then he shook his head again. "No."

"I know why," Lisa said. "You think you want a man to help Molly. But I can help Molly as much as any man can. Look at these muscles." She rolled up her sleeve and showed Mr. Brewster that her muscles were getting larger. As she did it she knew she was making a fool of herself. In the first place, though her muscles were bigger than they used to be, they were not very big. She had put on a little weight but she was still a tall, skinny kid.

Just as she feared, Mr. Brewster burst out laughing at her. Only, instead of telling her no again, he slapped his hand on his knee, he bent over double laughing, straightened up and said, "O.K., kiddo, you've got the job."

"I've got the job?" Lisa asked incredulously.

"Sure, you've got the job." He stopped laughing long enough to ask, "You did want the job, didn't you? You weren't just setting me up to sue me for not giving you equal opportunity?" Then he bent over double laughing again. "Now I've lost my first case to my first women's libber. Show me that muscle again."

Lisa sat in the chair, her face burning. She wasn't sure she even wanted the job if Mr. Brewster was going to make fun of her like this. Finally, she said, "I'll do good work."

Mr. Brewster stood up. He straightened out his face

93

and stopped laughing, though Lisa detected a smile that kept tugging at the corners of his eyes and mouth. He said, "Let's go tell Molly you're hired."

"Don't you want to check with her first?" Lisa asked.

"No, she and my son have both been pleading your case for a week," he answered. "I must admit it was hard for me to imagine you as being seriously interested. Most young girls . . . you're so beauti . . . never mind. I just wasn't thinking right. You're obviously entitled to the work if you can handle it."

He was leading her out to the work area of the florist shop. When they came close to Molly, he said, "All right, Ms. McGuire. Here's your new assistant. She's to work forty hours a week and get minimum wage. After a month, she goes up twenty-five cents an hour. And don't let me hear you complain if you have to do a lot of the heavy work yourself. You got the one you wanted."

Molly smiled at Lisa and asked, "How did you manage it?"

Lisa, remembering the scene in the office, doubled over with laughter. Now she could see how funny it really was. Finally, she gasped, "I showed him my muscles. He was very impressed."

9

Lisa loved working full time in the flower shop. Molly was fun to work with, and Lisa loved working with the flowers. Even though most of her tasks were difficult and dirty, she never complained. Of course the best part of the job was that she got to see Rick, but she would have loved the work anyway.

Mr. Brewster still made her slightly uncomfortable, but he wasn't around very much. He owned two other shops in smaller towns and spent a lot of time visiting those. The rest of the time, he worked in his office or was out visiting clients.

The day-to-day work was supervised by Molly, who seemed to be everywhere, doing everything. Lisa was her assistant and worked directly under her, doing whatever she was told. Most of the work was sorting, cleaning, straightening, lifting or carrying, and Lisa knew she was getting stronger and healthier every day.

She developed a tremendous appetite, and the others began to tease her about the big lunches she carried to work. But Lisa didn't mind, because her mirror told her she was putting weight on in the right places. Not only was she getting rounder, but she was feeling better than she'd ever felt in her life.

Besides Rick and Molly, there were three other people who worked in the shop. She liked them all, even though she didn't feel as close to them as she did to Molly. Linda, a tall, heavy and slow older woman, worked in the greenhouses taking care of the young flowers and plants. She had masses of curly gray hair and a slow, sweet smile. Most of the time she moved carefully and slowly down the long, straight rows of bedding plants or household shrubs. Lisa was sure that Linda's careful attentions were much of the reason that the Brewster flower shop had such healthy plants.

If Linda was slow and careful, Mike was just the opposite. He was a small, energetic man who smoked cigars and ran in and out, always seeming to be in a hurry. He lost a lot of things, and when he was around, the shop was filled with nervous confusion. However, Mike was cheerful and fun to be with, so Lisa didn't mind dropping her own work to help him find the bill or list that he'd put down somewhere. Mike's job was to do the maintenance and deliver orders. When Rick was working, as he was this summer, Mike spent a lot of time painting and repairing the buildings. Like Mr. Brewster, he was often in the other two shops, and part of his work was to see that the smaller shops were well stocked with cut flowers and decorative plants to sell.

The third worker, Helen, was a salesperson and bookkeeper. Since she was very quiet, Lisa felt as though she knew her the least of all. Even though she was always around, it was easy to overlook her, especially when Mike and Molly were there. Molly and Mike laughed and joked a lot. For that matter, so did Rick. After she'd been there a week, Lisa picked up the habit of making little jokes and teasing her fellow workers as well. It was fun.

Of all her chores, Lisa loved unwrapping the cut flowers more than anything else. When she came in at nine in the morning, Molly was already there and usually busy working on a special order for a funeral or a wedding. Sometimes she helped Molly a few minutes, all the time watching the talented woman work. Her secret dream was to be allowed to work on the arrangements, but she never dared suggest it. She had been hired to do the dirty work so Molly could do the decorations.

Around nine o'clock Rick would come into the shop, carrying a huge cardboard carton he'd picked up at the airport. Often there were several cartons, so Lisa would follow him out to the panel truck and stagger back to the shop with a cumbersome box of her own. Not only were the boxes large, about six feet long and eighteen inches wide, but they were a little heavy.

After she'd carried three or four of the boxes, Lisa would marvel at how heavy flowers could be. But she didn't really mind, because the next part of the work was her favorite part of the day. She and Rick would cut the bands on the large cardboard boxes, lift back the tops and pull off the tissue paper or covering of · newspaper. Underneath, they would find bundles of beautiful, fresh-cut flowers.

Most of the flowers were wrapped in bright green

tissue paper. Lisa didn't think she'd ever seen anything any lovelier than the first time she'd pulled back the fresh green paper and looked down at dozens and dozens of yellow gladiola blossoms lying like jewels on green velvet. Sometimes there would be whole boxes of one color and sometimes they would be mixed. Each package was different, and Lisa never got used to the magical moment.

She would pull back the covering, draw in her breath and say softly, "Look, pompoms," or "Oh, pink carnations!" Rick would laugh at her and tease. "Your favorites, right?"

Always Lisa would nod her head staunchly and insist that the flowers in front of her were her favorites. In a way, that was the truth, because Lisa loved all the flowers so much that she really couldn't make up her mind. She loved to think about them being cut the day before in some remote South American or Mexican village, carried to the airport in donkey-pulled carts and flown to Hartford, Connecticut, before dawn.

Not all the flowers came by airplane and not all of them came from Latin America, but that was the way they got most of their supply. Molly told her that in the winter every flower had to be specially shipped that way. Since this was summertime, some of the flowers came from local growers in New York and Pennsylvania.

Wherever they came from, Lisa loved the flowers, but unwrapping the boxes in the morning was an extra treat. It was a little like getting a Christmas present each morning. Sometimes the larger flowers were wrapped in newspaper with little newspaper collars or caps to protect the blooms. Sometimes there were very special flowers such as orchids or birds of paradise. But most of the blooms they used were pompoms, carnations, roses or statice. The big arrangements usually had a lot of gladiola blossoms in them.

But whether it was a small bunch of baby's breath or a dozen roses, Lisa loved equally the ones she was unwrapping. She and Rick would lift them out, cut off the bottoms of the stems, strip some of the lower leaves and put them in buckets of the right height. As she'd learned on her first day, fitting the flowers into the right height bucket was very important. If the bucket was too short, the flowers would flop over and lose their stem strength. A too tall bucket could drown the flowers. One of her favorite moments of the day was standing back after filling all the buckets and looking at the day's shipping of blossoms.

One day, there were about thirty buckets of flowers. She and Rick had been working hard for a long time, and now they were finished with that part of the job. Lisa straightened up, put her hands on her hips and stood smiling at the masses of pink and red blossoms in front of her.

"You must be Ferdinand's cousin," Rick said.

Lisa turned slowly. She didn't understand what he was saying at all. When he didn't explain, she asked, "Who's Ferdinand?"

"Didn't you read *Ferdinand the Bull* when you were a kid?" he asked.

"No."

"What? No Ferdinand? You had a deprived childhood," Rick teased.

The next day, he brought an old, worn copy of *Ferdinand the Bull* in to work. As he handed it to her he said, "I'll loan it to you. But I have to have it back. My little brother Benjie thinks the book was written especially for the Brewster family. He still reads it a lot."

Lisa took the children's book from him and read it on her lunch hour. It was a very cute story about a bull who didn't want to fight in the ring. All he wanted to do was smell the flowers. She enjoyed looking at the pictures and thought the story was funny. But most of all she enjoyed the fact that Rick had brought it to her. He must be a little interested, she told herself that afternoon as she carried pitchers of water from one part of the shop to the other, refilling the water in the cut-flower displays scattered around the different areas.

When Rick came in from his deliveries at four, she gave him back the book, thanking him. "Now my childhood is complete," she said. "I can truthfully say it was a good one. Before I met you, I only *thought* it was good."

When Rick laughed, she joined in easily. She was really very happy at the way she'd grown so relaxed around him. It helped a lot to work beside someone, and the best part was that the more she knew Rick, the better she liked him.

Of course, a lot of her good feelings faded when Patty came into the shop later that afternoon. Though Lisa felt she looked prettier than she'd ever looked, it always made her feel bad to compare herself to Patty. That afternoon, Patty was wearing a white tennis dress with a little short skirt. Her blond hair was tied back with a white ribbon, and she looked cool, cute and happy.

"Hi, Lisa," she said. "I just came by to steal Rick from you. Will you be able to close up without him?"

Rick hit his hand against his forehead and said, "I forgot." Then he turned to Lisa and said, "I'm sorry. I told Patty I'd ask you if I could leave early today. We're going to the lake to swim. Can you manage without me?"

Lisa tried to make her smile bright. "Sure."

"Good," Patty said. Then she added, "See you at the picnic Friday."

Lisa felt her heart sink. She'd been looking forward to the Brewster Fourth of July picnic ever since she'd heard about it. All the employees and their families were invited to a big picnic at the state forest. There would be a keg of beer, ham and hot dogs and prizes and games. Somehow, when she'd dreamed of the picnic, she'd imagined herself close to Rick. It had never occurred to her that Patty would be there, too.

As she watched Rick and Patty leave the shop and climb into Patty's bright red sports car, she decided to invite John as her date. She would feel better if John were tagging along, telling her how wonderful she was. Maybe it would ease the ache she felt each time she thought of Rick and Patty.

But when she asked John if he wanted to come to the picnic, he looked hurt and confused. He said, "Don't you remember that you told me it was only for employees? When you couldn't go out with me on the Fourth, I asked someone else. I'm sorry."

"It's not your fault," Lisa said. "I guess I was just sort of mixed up." But underneath her cheerful acceptance, Lisa was really a little annoyed with John for not offering to break the date. She would never let him do that, of course, but she was put out and surprised that he didn't offer. For the first time, Lisa was slightly jealous of whoever it was that John dated when she wouldn't go out with him. She had to bite her tongue to keep from asking who John was taking out and where they were going.

Poor John looked upset and sorry all evening. Eventually, Lisa got tired of hearing him apologize and said, "I want to go home. I'm tired and I want to go to sleep."

"But it's only ten o'clock," John said. "We haven't even heard a whole set of music."

"Got to get up early," Lisa reminded him. Then she yawned widely and John stood up, leaving the Cokes on the table and not even complaining about the cost of the short evening.

Though she knew it wasn't his fault, Lisa was more annoyed than ever with John that night and she promised herself once again that she would stop dating him. As she closed the door firmly in his face, avoiding a good-night kiss, she was sure that going out with John was worse than not going out at all. It wasn't that John was so bad, it was that he wasn't Rick.

But the day of the picnic Lisa honestly wished that she'd arranged things so that John had been with her. It hurt a lot to see Rick and Patty holding hands and laughing happily together. Lisa spent most of the time helping Molly and Mr. Brewster prepare the food. Once, Molly said, "You know, you're supposed to be out there with the rest of the folks, having a good time. I get paid good money to do this, and he owns the joint." She pointed to Adam Brewster, who was stirring a large pot of beans with a long wooden-handled spoon.

"Please let me help," Lisa said quickly.

Molly gave her one sharp, pitying glance and then said, "Torch carrying is hard work; maybe you should try to get over it."

"Torch carrying?"

Molly laughed. "Torch carrying is an old expression for holding on to a love for someone who doesn't love you. They used to call women singers who sang those sad love songs torch singers. I guess I'm showing my age when I tell you stuff like this."

Lisa, who was feeling embarrassed by the whole conversation, could think of nothing to say. She was glad when Adam Brewster called to Molly to come and help him.

Lisa continued putting out the paper plates and things. While she worked she watched Molly and Mr. Brewster working together. They laughed and joked and looked as happy as Patty and Rick. For the first time, Lisa wondered if it was possible that Molly and Mr. Brewster were interested in each other. Or was she imagining that the short, red-haired Molly's cheeks burned brighter when Adam Brewster was around? She decided to ask Molly if she were carrying a torch of her own when she came back.

But she didn't get a chance to ask Molly much of anything, because the others began drifting in from their games and walks with hungry looks on their faces. Very soon she was busy helping serve people. She was pleased to see that Rick had left Patty and stationed himself behind the hot dogs. He, too, worked until everyone else had been served. Then he walked over to Lisa and said, "Let's get something to eat and join Patty."

Lisa could do nothing but pick up a plate and follow

along behind Rick as he loaded her plate with hot dogs, potato salad, baked beans, coleslaw, pickles and olives. Finally, when she saw how much food he'd given her, she laughed. "You must really think I'm hungry."

Rick, who was looking directly into her eyes, said with a straight face, "I bet you eat it. Want to bet?"

Lisa felt her face flush, not because Rick was teasing her—she was used to that—but because he stood so close to her. She could feel his breath on her neck and he was looking directly into her eyes. Lisa always felt a warmth, a rush of tenderness, when she looked into Rick's rich brown eyes, but today the feeling was stronger then it had ever been. For a moment, she felt slightly dizzy and closed her eyes.

When she opened them, Rick's expression had changed. His face wore a slightly puzzled look. "You look beautiful," he said. Then, as though he were surprised at his own words, he amended the statement, trying to pass it off as a joke. "Beautiful and hungry. Let's go."

But Lisa's heart was racing with happiness and she knew she had heard what he'd said the first time. It was no joke. For one moment at least, Rick Brewster had seen her and said she was beautiful. For the first time all day, she was truly happy. Rick had called her beautiful! Life was good.

Patty looked annoyed when they joined her at the picnic table. That made Lisa feel good too, because she knew that Patty would never allow herself to look annoyed if she weren't really upset. Patty Baker was too cool, too composed and too collected to ever let on that she was worried about anything. But for at least a few minutes she seemed angry.

If Rick noticed that Patty was mad, he didn't react to it. He talked lightly of the picnic and the baseball game he had just finished pitching. When they'd finished eating, Rick said, "I guess I'd better go help Molly and my dad clean up."

That was when Patty exploded. "Really!" she said. "I think you could spend this last day with me. You know your father said you didn't have to work."

Rick smiled at Patty and said, "I'll be back in a little while. Come on, Lisa. Let's get to work."

"This is the end!" Patty said. "My last day in town and you spend it with . . ." She didn't seem to know how to end her sentence.

Lisa could no longer contain her curiosity. "Why is this your last day?"

Patty didn't act as though she'd heard her, but Rick said, "Patty is going to Colorado for two months. I'm going to be all alone." Then he tried for a smile as he said, "Course, I'll have you, Lisa."

"That's it!" Patty said. She threw her plate on the ground and walked away from the picnic table.

Lisa and Rick watched her march through the tables and off to the empty meadow that was part of the big park. Lisa's heart was beating so fast that she almost couldn't get the words out of her mouth. "You go get her, Rick. I'll help Molly and your dad."

Rick looked at Patty's retreating figure for a moment. Lisa was sure he was trying to decide what to do. She found she was holding her breath. Wouldn't it be wonderful if he were to decide to stay here with her? What if he let Patty keep on walking forever? Wouldn't that be wonderful?

"O.K.," Rick said. "Thanks a lot." Then, without

turning to look at Lisa at all, he broke into a run and starting calling to Patty. By the time he caught up with Patty, they looked like small dolls to Lisa.

Blinking back the tears of disappointment in her eyes, Lisa watched them talking for a few minutes, then went over to help Molly and Adam Brewster. As she walked toward the long table, Patty and Rick joined hands and ran lightly up and over a hill. By the time Lisa joined Molly, Rick and Patty were out of sight.

As she worked, Lisa went over the day's happenings in her mind. She couldn't help being excited about Rick and hoping for the best. After all, he'd told her she was beautiful, hadn't he? As for the fact that Patty was leaving for two months, Lisa could only be hopeful about that. Two months might just give her the time she needed to prove to Rick that he needed a new girl-friend.

As she thought these thoughts she worked at the long picnic table, stacking plates, closing and covering food and generally cleaning up. She didn't even notice that Molly and Mr. Brewster were gone until she saw the crowd of people gathered on one side of the picnic table area. Next, she thought she heard someone say, "She's really hurt."

Lisa put a lid over the potato salad and started walking toward the area where the others were gathered. But before she'd gone very far, she saw the crowd part in the middle and watched Adam Brewster carrying Molly toward the benches. Mr. Brewster, who wasn't a very tall man, struggled under the load of Molly's ample, though short, body. But Lisa saw that when Mike offered to help, Mr. Brewster shook his head and motioned for Mike to move away.

Staggering, he carried Molly from the benches to his

car, which was parked in a nearby parking lot. Before
Lisa had really understood exactly what had happened,
Adam Brewster and Molly McGuire were driving
away. "Where are they going?" Lisa asked no one in
particular.

"To the hospital. She's probably broken her leg,"
Mike answered.

10

Molly's leg wasn't broken, but her ankle was sprained so severely that the doctor said she couldn't work for at least a week. When Lisa went to see her at the hospital that evening, she seemed really upset by the news. "You'll have to fill in for me," Molly said. "That is, Adam and you will have to do my work." Then she sighed a great sigh and added, "I guess you'll have to call the Northeastern Flower Show and say we won't be entering this year, Adam."

Mr. Brewster was sitting beside Molly's bed. He said, "Look, Molly, you don't worry about the shop. Worry about getting well. Lisa and I will take care of the shop."

Lisa felt funny to have the two adults talk about depending on her in that way. She wondered if they really meant it or if they were just including her to be nice. She said, "I'll try and help."

"You always help," Adam Brewster said. "Nice girl. You're a nice girl, Lisa. Mike tells me that you and he cleaned up the picnic. That no-good son of mine disappeared."

Lisa flushed. "Rick didn't know that Molly was hurt. He and Patty—"

"Yeah, yeah. He's so silly about that girl that he isn't reliable anymore. Not sensible. That's what I told him last week." Adam Brewster snorted and continued, "Can you imagine? Wants to take two weeks off in the middle of summer and hitchhike to Colorado? So silly about that girl he doesn't even think straight."

Perhaps because she saw the pain in Lisa's face, Molly interrupted. "Adam, will you go get me a magazine before the gift shop closes? If I'm really going to have to spend the night in this joint, I may as well have something to entertain me."

"You shouldn't spend all night reading," Adam Brewster grumbled, but he rose from the chair and obediently left the room.

Molly said to Lisa, who was fighting to keep back the tears, "Look, kiddo, don't pay too much attention to what Adam says. He's like that—always complaining about Rick. He doesn't _know_ that Rick is that silly about Patty."

"No, he's right," Lisa said. "Rick is crazy about Patty. I know it and I haven't wanted to face it. But Mr. Brewster is right; Rick can't really see straight when Patty is around."

Molly reached out and patted Lisa's hand. "I'm sorry. You're a much nicer girl, you know. Prettier, too."

Lisa smiled at her boss and friend in gratitude. It helped to have that sort of support from people, but she knew it wasn't true. Patty Baker was a lot prettier than she was, though maybe not any nicer. "It doesn't really matter," Lisa said. "You can't pick who you fall for. Look at John. John Reesner is crazy about me and I'm not interested in him."

Molly laughed. "There, you see! You're not the loser you think you are. Got one young man following you around like a puppy dog, and there will be others. Believe me, Lisa, you'll have plenty of chances."

Lisa didn't know what to answer to that. She knew if she told Molly that she was sure Rick was the only boy she'd ever want, Molly would think she was silly. Older people had a way of thinking that kids couldn't feel anything very deeply. Yet Lisa was sure that her feeling for Rick was a true one. She was not a silly person and her feelings were real.

Fortunately, she didn't have to say anything else to Molly, because Mr. Brewster came back into the room, carrying a stack of magazines and a box of candy.

Molly's face lit up when she saw him, and for the second time Lisa wondered if Molly's affection for her boss was more than it seemed on the surface. She decided to let the two of them have the rest of visiting hours together, just in case, and rose to go home.

Molly said, "You'll have to call Northeastern tomorrow. I hate to do it, but Adam will have too much to do without worrying about entering a silly contest."

"We'll enter," Adam Brewster growled. "Brewster Florist has entered the Northeastern Flower Show for ten years. We're not going to default now."

Molly shook her head in dismay. As Lisa left the room the two adults were arguing in their usual manner. Lisa smiled as she walked down the corridor of the hospital. If that was love, they had a funny way of showing it. Besides, she'd never seen any signs that Mr. Brewster was interested in Molly. And Molly's cheerful look whenever he came in the room might be no more than her happy disposition. Still, it might be nice. . . .

During the next few days, Lisa found it easier to think about Molly and her possible romance than to think about Rick. Rick was obviously very upset because Patty was gone. He moped around the shop, looking absolutely miserable. He forgot things, never laughed and seemed to be far away most of the time. Even Lisa had to agree with his father that Rick wasn't being much help in this time of emergency. With Molly gone, it would have been easier if Rick had been his usual cheerful and helpful self, but Lisa didn't blame him. She tried to do her own and as much of Molly's and Rick's work as she could so that Mr. Brewster wouldn't be so angry at his son.

But Lisa couldn't do much to cover Rick's mistakes, and he made plenty of them. By the end of the week, Lisa had to admit to herself that Rick was never going to be interested in anyone except Patty. She forced herself to quit dreaming about the time when Rick would look up from the work he was doing and see her. Rick saw her, all right—he saw her as a nice kid.

Most of that week, she was working too hard to worry about her feelings for Rick, though she did promise herself that she'd stop hoping. When John called and asked her out two times in the same week, she didn't put him off. Instead, she told him sweetly that she'd love to go. She forced herself to be nicer to John, at least partly because she had some idea of what he was feeling. In his heart, John must know that his love for Lisa was hopeless, just as Lisa knew her love for Rick was hopeless.

Sadness made her gentle, and to tell the truth, she was grateful that John was still around. The summer would have been terrible without his wistful smile and loving attention. They went to the beach on her day off and she had a good time.

She was lying on a big yellow towel, looking at the people dive off the end of the pier, when John told her how he felt about her. "I know you know this, Lisa but I have to say it anyway. I want you to be my girl. I want us to be a couple. I want you to be beside me all the time. I want . . ."

Lisa laughed and rolled over lazily, looking at John's sweet face. She reached up one hand and put it over his mouth, saying, "I want . . . I want. . . . John, you should hear how you sound. Don't rush me, please."

His face clouded and he said quickly, "I'm sorry, Lisa. I guess I got carried away. The truth is, when I'm with you, I get sort of tongue-tied. I always seem to say and do the wrong thing. I'm sorry."

Lisa laughed louder this time. "Now your record is stuck again. Before it was 'I want, I want'; now it's 'I'm sorry, I'm sorry,'" she teased.

John looked down. Lisa knew she was being mean to tease him like this, but it gave her a feeling of power. Even if Rick wasn't interested in her, she could make another fellow do flip-flops. She was a little surprised at the feeling, but she had to admit she liked it.

When John said, "I'm sorry," one more time, Lisa laughed and got up.

She ran to the lake, calling back to him, "Come on in, the water's fine." John followed her, of course, and they spent the rest of the afternoon swimming and lying on the floating deck, talking to other kids.

Angela was on the float when John and Lisa swam

up. Lisa climbed on board and said, "Hi, Angela, how are you?"

Angela seemed not to hear Lisa because she was busy turning to dive off the other end. As Lisa watched her old friend swim off she said softly, "I wish I knew what was wrong with her. I can't figure out why she's mad at me."

"Angela's not mad at you," John said quietly. "I think it's because I stopped calling her so much."

"You've been dating Angela a lot?" Lisa asked. She was surprised at the funny tug of jealousy as she asked the question. How could she be so crazy about Rick and yet jealous of John?

"Not a lot," John said. Then he added, "Since you've stopped putting me off so much, I've stopped dating anyone else."

Lisa had so many mixed feelings at that remark that she didn't know what to say. On the one hand, she really wasn't interested in John. On the other hand, she was glad he was around to fill in the empty time. She knew that watching Rick with Patty would be a lot harder if she didn't have John in tow. As she watched her old friend Angela swim away she wondered if she would ever get her feelings together again.

At least at work she was too busy to worry much about her love life. Rick was just as sad and useless as ever when she went in the next day. For once, she actually agreed with his father's point of view. It seemed to Lisa that Rick could make more of an effort to get himself together. After all, Patty was only going to be gone two months. That wasn't forever.

Lisa didn't say anything to Rick about the way she felt. In fact, she didn't see as much of Rick that week as she usually did. She'd promised herself she'd forget

Rick after listening to Mr. Brewster complain about his obsession with Patty. Because she was really trying to let go of her own obsession with Rick, she consciously tried to avoid him. In a way it was easy, because Mr. Brewster, who was taking on much of Molly's work, seemed to like having her around.

She really got so she liked Mr. Brewster a lot. He grumbled and groaned but he always treated her well. Often, he complained to Lisa about his sons, but Lisa could tell that he really loved both boys a lot. One day, while they were working on a funeral arrangement together, Mr. Brewster said, "I haven't had it easy, you know. Raising two boys all alone isn't any picnic. Their mother died when they were young. Since then, I've been mother and father to them. It isn't easy."

"Maybe you should marry," Lisa ventured. She was thinking of Molly's bright eyes each time Adam Brewster came in the room.

Adam Brewster snorted and grumped. "No time to meet a good woman. No time for singles swinging." Then he laughed and confided, "Right after my wife died, friends tried to fix me up with some nice ladies. But I wasn't ready. Now, everyone thinks of me as a happy bachelor." He frowned, "Besides, I'd feel silly dating. Got a son who's dating age. I'd feel like a fool."

"Marry someone you know," Lisa suggested. She held her breath, waiting for Mr. Brewster to tell her to mind her own business, but he seemed very intent on getting the gladiolas to lie flat beside the huge purple ribbon. If he heard her suggestion, or knew whom she had in mind, he didn't acknowledge it.

Later that afternoon, Mr. Brewster worked a long time on a bouquet of summer flowers. He fussed and fussed with the design, pulling blossoms off and substituting others. Lisa wondered if he was practicing for the Northeastern Flower Show which they would enter tomorrow. Finally, he seemed satisfied with his bouquet of red roses and white pompoms. He picked up the flowers and said, "I'll see you tomorrow morning. You can close up without me."

Lisa hoped with all her heart that the flowers were for Molly. She knew that Mr. Brewster had been to visit Molly twice since she'd come home from the hospital. Just in case there was a chance that Mr. Brewster was really carrying those flowers over to Molly's house, Lisa called her friend and said that she'd not be able to come by after work.

Molly said, "Oh, I miss work. But the doctor said I can't come in till next Tuesday. That's almost two weeks."

"It isn't the same without you," Lisa said. Then she told Molly all about the day's work.

"You'll be working on the entries for the Northeastern Flower Show tomorrow," Molly said. "Adam says he's going to let you do two of them and he'll do the other three. I hope you win a prize."

"I wish he wouldn't do that," Lisa said. "I know he's just trying to be nice. I'm not really good enough to enter a flower show."

"Just keep it simple," Molly advised. "Your work is as good as most florists' who've been in the business for years."

They talked for a few minutes more. Lisa knew she should hang up the phone and get started closing up the shop, but she couldn't help hoping that while she was talking Mr. Brewster would come to Molly's house. Sure enough, just as Lisa said, "I guess I should . . ." the doorbell rang and Molly told her to hang on.

Lisa was surprised at how excited she was as she waited for Molly to come back to the telephone. When Molly said, "Lisa . . ." over the wire, Lisa asked, "Is it Mr. Brewster?"

"How did you know?"

Lisa laughed delightedly. "Oh, Molly, I think you've got a boyfriend! Is he holding a big bouquet of flowers?"

Molly's voice was an embarrassed whisper as she said, "Don't be silly, Lisa. Now I'm going to hang up."

"Have fun," Lisa said but Molly had already hung up.

Lisa's eyes were shining and she was smiling as she began running around the florist shop, sweeping up for the last time and getting ready to close the doors. The idea that Mr. Brewster and Molly might be having a romance appealed to her very much. She just hoped it were true.

For the first time since Patty left town, Rick was cheerful. He said, "You look like the understudy who's ready for her big break. Understand you're going to do some of the arrangements for tomorrow's show?"

"Yes. But I didn't really want Molly to sprain her ankle," Lisa answered promptly. It was nice to have the old banter back between them.

"Then how come you look like the cat who ate the canary?"

Lisa thought about telling Rick about Molly and his father and decided against it. She was sure she was right, but it wouldn't help Molly to tell Rick. No matter what Rick thought about Molly, his dad wouldn't appreciate any interference. She said, "I'm just glad to be alive today."

Rick leaned on his broom and looked at her meditatively. He said, "You do look glad."

It was a small exchange but it cheered Lisa up a lot. Even though she'd decided to drop her hopes about Rick as a boyfriend, she hated to see him in such a black mood. She hoped the good mood would last.

But the next day, when Lisa and Mr. Brewster worked on the arrangements for the show, Rick was as gloomy as ever. His father tried to get him to help with the big entry but Rick said, "Not me. I'm not talented and I'm not in the mood."

"You're in some kind of mood," his father grumbled. "Why can't you be cheerful and helpful like Lisa?"

Lisa blushed a bright red and bent over her small bouquet of daisies. It bothered her a lot to hear Mr. Brewster pick on Rick. Worst of all, she hated to have him use her as an example of any sort. She hoped that Rick wouldn't hate her for his father's comparison.

Rick didn't answer. In fact, he walked away and didn't come close to them until it was time to load the flower arrangements on the truck to take to the show.

As he picked up the arrangements he said, "Is this all?"

Lisa felt her heart sink. Rick obviously was not impressed with the two small arrangements she'd done. As for Mr. Brewster's two bigger ones, even she could see that they were not his best work. She'd been surprised that Mr. Brewster had seemed so uninterested this morning. All he'd really done was a simple floral arrangement that he used a lot for funerals. In fact, Lisa was sure it was not as good as the average design Brewster Florist sent out for Mother's Day.

She didn't expect to win any prizes and she was

pretty sure that Mr. Brewster's entries wouldn't win anything either. So it was with great surprise that she answered the telephone later that day to hear Rick's voice calling long distance.

He and his father had made the trip to Hartford for the show. Mr. Brewster had apologized that he couldn't take her along too. He'd said, "If you win, we'll call you."

Now here was Rick on the other end of the telephone, saying, "You won first prize in the under-fifteen-dollars category. For the daisies."

"Really?" Lisa couldn't believe it. Her little arrangement had seemed so ordinary.

"Yes. Your daisies were the only thing that won anything. You should be proud. Dad says you get a twenty-dollar bonus. For the publicity, you know. He says take it out of the till tonight."

"Oh, Rick, I couldn't."

"Sure you can," Rick said. "Just go to the cash register, ring the no-sale key and lift twenty dollars. Put it in your pocket and walk away. Be sure and close the drawer," he teased. Then he said, "I'm glad for you, Lisa. You deserve a prize. You'll get a ribbon and the store will get a plaque to hang with the others in the office."

"The ribbon will be nice," Lisa said. "But I can't take money for doing my job."

"Go ahead and take it," Rick said. "You can take John out for a change. He spends plenty of money on you, doesn't he? Give the guy a break."

As Lisa hung up the telephone she was as full of mixed feelings as ever. She was delighted to have the prize, of course. She was even glad it was Rick who had called her instead of Mr. Brewster. Had he asked for the privilege? she wondered. But his reference to taking John out had shown her once and for all that he wasn't interested in her. No fellow would suggest such a thing if he had even a slight interest in a girl, would he?

Lisa drew in her breath and turned toward the cash register. She'd promised herself that she wouldn't carry the torch for Rick any longer, hadn't she? Yet here she was, still thinking about him and his lack of interest in her. Well, she wasn't going to keep on with that nonsense. No, she wasn't. She was a winner. She would show Rick Brewster—she would do exactly as he suggested. She would take John out to dinner and the movies with her money. And what's more, she would have a good time.

11

When Molly came back on Tuesday, Lisa was sure the woman was in love. Molly was wearing a new print shirt and had her red hair tied back with a bright yellow band. Instead of the usual worn Levi's, she was wearing polyester slacks and new white tennis shoes. "You look pretty," Lisa said.

All Molly said was thanks, and Lisa was sure she didn't want to be questioned too closely about her feelings or what was going on between her and Mr. Brewster. Lisa talked about the shop, filling Molly in on the orders and the bookwork that were waiting for her. She said, "I guess Mr. Brewster and I didn't really do all your work, did we? Seems like we left an awful lot for you. I'm sorry."

"Don't be sorry," Molly said. "You did a good job. And congratulations on the prize. What did you do with the money?"

"Took my . . . took a boy I date out to the pizza parlor and the movies. It went fast." Lisa had been a little surprised at the amount of money she'd spent in that one evening and she'd wondered how John always seemed to find the cash to take her out. It had made Lisa a little uncomfortable to think about all the money he must have spent on her in the last year.

She didn't tell Molly any of those feelings. In fact, they were both so busy the next few days that they didn't talk much at all. It was Friday before Molly had her desk cleared off. About two o'clock, Molly said, as casually as possible, "Lisa, I'm taking off for a couple of hours this afternoon. Watch the shop for me?"

"Sure," Lisa said. "Got a doctor's appointment?"

"No."

The shortness of Molly's answer made Lisa more curious than ever. When Molly came back with her bright red hair curled and twisted into a sophisticated hairdo, Lisa's curiosity was satisfied. "You had your hair done," she said. "It looks wonderful."

"Really?" Molly asked. "Not too fancy?"

"Really. It makes you look taller and thinner. Very sophisticated," Lisa assured her. "Going someplace special?"

Molly nodded her head, and Lisa was pretty sure she wasn't going to volunteer any more than that. Then Molly bit her lip nervously and said, "Promise you won't tell Mike or anyone else? I couldn't stand it if they teased me."

"You're going out with Mr. Brewster, aren't you?" Lisa said. "Oh, Molly, I'm so happy for you. He's really a very nice man and he's almost good enough for you."

"Careful, kiddo. I'm going to dinner, not to the

121

altar," Molly said quickly. "I almost turned him down. It doesn't really do to mix business with pleasure, as you know. Oh . . . I didn't mean you and Rick . . . I was just talking. . . . I guess I'd better shut up."

Lisa had never seen Molly so nervous. She felt kind of sorry for her friend and at the same time was amused to see that adults could get just as flustered and nervous as teenagers when it came to dating and romance. "I just hope you have a good time," Lisa said. "You deserve it."

"Thanks," Molly said. "How about you? Do you have a date tonight?"

"Not tonight," Lisa answered quickly. She didn't tell Molly that she'd told John she was too busy redecorating her bedroom to go to the movies. Even when she'd given John the excuse, she'd known it was a silly one. Like her parents, Molly thought John was a nice boy and didn't like to think of Lisa being mean to him. Well, John was a nice boy, but she still wasn't very enthusiastic about him.

Lisa knew she should try to appreciate John's wonderful qualities, and she did, but she also knew that he just wasn't the guy for her. Even though she'd made a real effort to forget Rick, she was still much more attracted to him than to John. Maybe Rick wasn't the one for her, but whoever that special fellow would be, it would not be John.

As Lisa was thinking these thoughts she was sweeping for the last time that day, gathering together the small scraps of ribbon, bits of leaf and dust that the day's activities accumulated. She was so deep in thought that she didn't notice when Rick and Mike came into the workroom. They were arguing about a lost bill. As usual, Mike was insisting that he'd never seen it and that Rick must have had it earlier in the day.

Rick, trying to keep the irritation out of his voice, said, "Forget it, Mike. We'll get the duplicate from the desk. I'll make a copy, and when we come across the original, we'll replace the copy."

"All right," Mike grumbled. "But you should try not to be so careless."

Lisa giggled and looked at Rick, who winked at her. He grinned and said, "All right, Mike. I'll try to be more careful in the future. More like you are."

Mike didn't hear the sarcasm in Rick's voice and went home, apparently happy to have won the argument about who had lost the bill. Rick, who didn't seem very upset, went over to the desk, pulled out the order pad and began copying the order over.

When he finished, he looked up and said to Lisa, "Want to go out for hamburgers with me tonight?"

"Tonight?" Lisa couldn't believe she'd heard what she'd heard. She'd dreamed it so often that now that it was happening she couldn't really believe it.

"Maybe you already have a date. Or maybe you don't go out with anyone but John. You don't have to think of it as a date at all, if you don't want to," Rick said. "I'm just going to be lonely tonight. My kid brother went away for a weekend camping with the Scouts. My dad has a date with Molly. I thought . . ." For once, Rick seemed a little unsure of himself and he trailed off without actually finishing his sentence.

"No," Lisa said quickly. Then she laughed and took a breath before she began explaining. "I mean no, I don't have a date. Yes, I'd love to have a hamburger with you."

Rick looked relieved as he said, "Great, I'll pick you up in an hour. O.K.?"

Lisa hurried to get the sweeping done, run home, change clothes and take a shower before the hour was up. When Rick drove up in the panel truck at six she was standing in the doorway, waiting for him. She quickly introduced him to her parents and they were out of the door.

Once in the truck, Rick said, "I'm really glad you could go with me. I would have been very hungry. You see, I can't cook and I hate to eat alone."

"Can't cook at all?" Lisa asked. "Not even a cheese sandwich?"

"Well, maybe a cheese sandwich," Rick conceded, "but it isn't the same as having a pretty girl for company."

Lisa told herself not to count on anything. She told herself over and over that just because Rick had asked her to have a hamburger with him, he didn't really have to be interested in her. She told herself that his girl was Patty and she was, at best, a second choice. In fact, he had made it very clear that he wouldn't have even asked her out if his father hadn't had a date.

Even though she tried to keep her expectations realistic, even though she told herself over and over not to count on too much, she had a wonderful time. Riding beside Rick in the truck was an exciting feeling. Once, when he turned a corner sharply, she leaned into his shoulder. Her shoulder touching his seemed like a kind of magical electricity. She caught her breath and straightened up quickly.

He laughed and said, "Sorry. The pickup doesn't ride as smoothly as the car, but my dad needed that." He laughed louder and added, "Poor Dad, he was so nervous. Old people can really get uptight about dates, I guess. Not that he's had many of them. I think taking Molly to dinner has been the only date he's had this year."

"Maybe it's serious," Lisa ventured.

"Maybe," Rick said. "But it's hard to tell. He was crazy about my mother. I never thought he'd get over it."

They talked in a general way about the flower shop, summer vacation and kids they knew at school. As they sat across from each other in Hamburger Haven, Rick stirred his coffee carefully. He said, "The summer is half over. You know, I never thought it would go so fast. But it's almost August. Six more weeks and school starts."

Lisa bit into her hamburger, thinking that Rick was probably counting the weeks until Patty returned. She could think of nothing to say, so she sat silently, waiting for Rick to continue his train of thought.

But if Rick was thinking of Patty, his face didn't show it. He seemed to be having a good time and suggested that they go to the movies after supper.

"Unless you have to get home," Rick said.

"No. All I have to do is work tomorrow," Lisa said. "I'm used to that."

They went to the movies, staying for both features, and laughing at the same silly jokes. It was midnight when they got out of the theater. As they walked to his truck, Rick took Lisa's hand and said, "Thanks, Lisa. You made my evening fun instead of lonely. Besides being pretty, you laugh at the same corny jokes that I do. I knew the minute I met you that you had class."

Lisa's hand felt warm and wonderful as it lay in Rick's. She was smiling in the dark. How many times had she dreamed of an evening like this? Now it was happening and it was wonderful, just as she'd always hoped it would be.

They didn't talk much on the way home from the movies, but the silence was comfortable. When they pulled up in front of her house, Lisa said, "I had a great time. Thanks for asking me."

Rick leaned over, put his arm around her and kissed her on the lips. It was a nice, soft kiss, but Lisa's response was as romantic as she'd always dreamed. Rick's lips on hers made her feel beautiful, exciting and wonderful.

She knew her voice was trembling as she said, "Good night, Rick. It was fun."

Instead of answering, Rick got out of the truck and came around to help her down. As they walked to her front door Lisa was conscious of the fact that they were exactly the same height. She'd never kissed anyone standing up but John, and John was almost four inches taller than she was. Would she feel awkward and embarrassed if Rick tried to kiss her again? She wasn't sure how you kissed a boy who was just your height. Should she lean her head to one side? But that would feel silly.

When they got to the front porch, Lisa pulled her hand away from Rick and practically ran to her front door. There, she paused and smiled what she hoped was a dazzling smile and said, "Thanks again, Rick. See you tomorrow."

She was inside the house before Rick had a chance to answer. Once inside, she burst into tears. She knew it was silly to be crying because Rick had kissed her, but she couldn't help it. The evening's excitement had been too much for her, she knew. First, she had been so busy trying to seem casual about the most important date of her life. Then she had responded so definitely to his kiss. Last, she'd made a complete fool of herself by running into the house like a twelve-year-old ninny.

Lisa knew the tears were partly a result of her emotions and partly because she was sure she'd never be asked out by Rick again. After a smooth, sophisticated girl like Patty Baker, she must have been a very poor second. Feeling very sorry for herself, Lisa went to her room and undressed for bed.

As she went to sleep she could still feel Rick's warm lips on hers. Nevertheless, quiet tears rolled down her cheeks. It had been a wonderful date, and at the same time it had been horrible. She was certain it was going to be her last with Rick Brewster. On that miserable thought, she fell asleep.

12

The next morning, when she went to work, Lisa was unhappy and depressed. Molly, however, was radiantly happy. Seeing so clearly that Molly's date had been a success only made Lisa more unhappy about her own. When Molly told her that Rick would be working in the Lenox store for the day, she was just as glad. She wouldn't have known how to act anyway.

Besides the main store in Wilmington, Brewster Florist had two smaller branches in small towns a few miles away. The branch stores sold cut flowers and plants and took orders for floral arrangements which were done in the big store. Part of Rick's job was to deliver plants and flowers to each of the smaller stores. Lisa knew he liked driving the truck more than working inside the shops, but she couldn't help wondering if he'd volunteered for the job today. Maybe Rick was just as uncomfortable about their date as she was.

She worked very hard all day long, and by late afternoon she was feeling dirty and tired. In fact, she'd had troubles that day that she hadn't had since the very first day on the job. When she knocked over a stack of buckets, rolling the big round tins around on the shop's floor, Molly looked up from her work and said, "What's wrong, Lisa? If I didn't know better, I'd say you were in love."

Instead of replying courteously, Lisa snapped, "You put the buckets in the wrong place. It was your fault!"

Immediately, Lisa was sorry she'd said such a thing. Though it was true that Molly had put the buckets in the wrong place, it was also true that she was the boss. You didn't snap at your boss if you wanted to keep your job, and Lisa loved her job. At least, most of the time she loved her work. Today she didn't love anything.

Molly didn't say anything to her except "Well, pick them up. Then you'd better take a break. Take half an hour off and get some ice cream to sweeten your disposition. It hasn't been exactly cheerful working with you today. You know, it's not my fault that Rick isn't here."

"That's not the reason," Lisa began to explain, but she stopped. What was the use? Molly would never understand. She didn't really understand herself why she felt so miserable. She tried to tell herself that even if she never dated Rick again, she wouldn't be any worse off than she had been before. She'd never really expected to go out with Rick even once, had she?

But as the day wore on and she didn't see or hear from Rick, she knew she was disappointed. Deep in her heart, she'd hoped that he would at least find time to call her. He must not have cared about her at all.

It was with a heavy heart that Lisa left Brewster

Florist and went home that Saturday afternoon. The weather didn't help her mood any. As she walked through the hot, muggy streets, she wished it would rain. The rain would be hot, but it would be good to get really wet. Right now, the air felt damp and steamy. She pushed her long black hair out of her eyes and blew upward on her forehead. Maybe, when she got home, she would persuade John to go down to the lake for a swim.

At the thought of John, tears began to roll down her cheeks again. She didn't want to go swimming with John. John was not Rick, and it was Rick that she wanted to be with this evening.

Thunder cracked and the skies poured hot rain down on the earth below. Lisa walked through the storm, letting the rain wash away some of the sadness as it cooled her off. By the time she got home, she was as wet as she'd ever been in her life but a little happier. She knew that somehow she would get through the weekend. Monday was her day off, and Tuesday she would talk to Rick. She would find some way to tell him that she didn't expect anything. She would find some way to get the relationship back to the nice, easygoing friendship it had been before.

By Tuesday, Lisa had prepared her speech at least a hundred times. In her mind, she'd gone over everything she could possibly think to say to Rick. She wanted to let him know that she didn't expect him to fall in love with her. She wanted to let him know that she was happy to be his friend. She wanted to let him know that she knew she could never compete with Patty Baker.

Lisa's hands were shaking as she cut open the first box of flowers that Rick brought in. If Rick noticed that she was nervous, he didn't say anything about it. He seemed exactly the same as he'd always been, calm and sure of himself. All he'd said as he came in the door was hello, but Lisa hadn't really expected him to say anything else.

She waited until they'd put all the flowers in the buckets and then she said quickly, "Rick, I had a nice time the other night, I really did, but I know . . . that is, I just think the most important thing is to be friends, don't you?"

Rick looked at her quietly for a moment. Then he said, "We are friends, Lisa. We've always been friends."

"It's just that I know it could never be anything serious . . . ." Lisa felt stiff and uncomfortable. As she talked she wondered where all the fancy words she'd so carefully prepared had flown. She knew she wasn't making much sense but she had to go on. "I mean, you're dating Patty . . ."

"And you're dating John," Rick finished. "O.K., Lisa, let's just leave it at that."

Rick turned and walked away from her as Lisa fought back tears. She told herself that she was getting to be a crybaby and forced herself to laugh and smile the rest of the day. By the end of the day, Rick was laughing and joking with her, and she congratulated herself for getting things back on a friendly basis. At least, if they couldn't be romantic friends, they could keep the friendship.

That afternoon, when she was getting ready to leave the shop, she said, "See you tomorrow, Rick."

"See you tomorrow, Lisa."

Just looking into Rick's warm brown eyes made Lisa feel good. She was glad that she had the job and could be close to him every day. In a way, just getting to know him better had been more than she'd hoped for a few months ago. She was a lucky girl, Lisa told herself. From now on, she was going to count her blessings, not worry about what she couldn't have.

But during the next week, she had a hard time counting her blessings. In spite of his initial friendliness, she was pretty sure that Rick was avoiding her. A couple of times she caught him looking at her when she wasn't supposed to know it. His face had a quizzical expression, and Lisa was afraid that his distance was really disapproval.

The more she thought about it, the more awkward she felt, so that by the end of the week she was really very tongue-tied around Rick. On Saturday afternoon he didn't say more than good night to her. If Lisa had held any hopes at all, they were gone now. She left Brewster Florist feeling almost as depressed as she had the week before.

That evening, she was cross with John, then immediately apologized. "John, I'm sorry. It's not your fault. It's this hot weather that's getting me down."

"Yeah, July was really a scorcher. I hope August is better." Then he dropped his arm around her shoulder and said, "Look, there's the August moon."

Lisa looked up at the bright yellow moon that seemed to be hanging over her house. It was a beautiful sight and she knew that it would be very romantic if she were with Rick. As it was, she was only annoyed by the reference to the date. Since this was August, that meant that Patty would be back in four and a half weeks. What was worse, she'd be finished with her job at Brewster Florist and back in school. This year, Rick would be a senior and only taking three classes. The rest of the time he would be working and she would never see him.

Lisa sighed and said. "Too bad you can't wish upon a moon."

"You can," John said. "You're so beautiful tonight. You know, you've always been beautiful, but this summer you're even more so. What have you done?"

Lisa laughed. It always felt good to have John around, telling her how wonderful or beautiful she was. She said, "I haven't done anything except work hard, eat more and get a tan."

"Whatever it was," John said as he brought his lips to her cheek.

Lisa drew back. "Honestly, all you think about is kissing. Let's talk."

John's face took on that hurt, humble look that Lisa hated. He always made her feel so guilty. As she had a hundred times, Lisa decided that she was going to stop dating John. She really didn't like him. But Lisa knew she wouldn't have the courage to drop John unless she had someone to take his place. She didn't want to have that old dateless and standing-on-the-sidelines feeling again. No, John might not be perfect, but he was someone. And someone was better than no one.

"What was your wish?" John asked. "Your wish upon the moon?"

"Can't tell," Lisa answered. "Wishes don't come true if you tell."

"I'll tell you mine," John offered.

Lisa laughed again. She was pretty sure that John was wishing something sappy about the two of them. She leaned over, kissed him lightly on the lips and hopped out of the car before he could protest or catch her.

As she ran to the door of her house she was still

laughing at the surprised look on poor John's face. If only she could learn to handle Rick with the ease she handled John, she thought. That was what she should have wished for. Instead, she had wished the same old wish. Though she didn't believe that Rick would ever be attracted to her if he hadn't been before now, she couldn't help wishing, could she? A girl had a right to wish and dream.

13

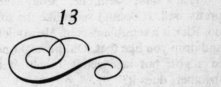

But no matter what her dreams were, Lisa had to face facts on Tuesday morning when she went back to work. Rick was friendly and nice, of course, but there was no doubt in Lisa's mind that things weren't the same as they'd been before the date. They worked together in polite silence most of the time, and most of the easy joking went on between the others. Neither Rick nor Lisa seemed to be able to find anything to say to each other.

Lisa was almost glad when Rick volunteered to take the funeral designs over to the mortuary and let Mike take an early coffee break. Though it was obvious that Rick was trying to stay away from her as much as he could, she was having so much difficulty talking with him that she didn't care. How had things become so strained between them?

Later that afternoon, Molly asked her what she was

thinking. She said, "What happened between you two? You don't seem very happy with each other anymore."

Instead of saying nothing or trying to pass it off, Lisa decided to talk to Molly. Maybe she could help her fix things. Lisa told her the whole story of the date and their conversation the day after.

Molly listened quietly, then questioned Lisa carefully about exactly what she had said to Rick. Lisa tried to tell her, but ended with, "It doesn't really matter, does it? The point is, Rick isn't interested in me. Now he doesn't even seem to like me anymore."

"That's what doesn't fit," Molly said. "I know Rick pretty well. It doesn't seem like the sort of thing he'd do. Rick is a sensible person. He wouldn't take you out and drop you like that. Oh, he might not be interested in a girl, but he's acting funny. It just doesn't fit together, does it?"

Lisa had to admit as she listened to Molly's objections that there was something wrong with the way she'd told the story. She must have misunderstood some part of the evening. She said to Molly, "All I know for sure is that Rick is acting funny around me."

"And you're acting funny around him."

"Yes, but that's because I'm in love with him," Lisa said. It sounded good to finally say the word *love* out loud. One good thing about Molly was that she would never laugh at someone for saying a word like *love*.

"Maybe Rick's in love with you, too," Molly suggested.

"Don't be silly."

"Think about it," Molly went on. "Maybe you were so sure that Rick wouldn't be interested that you didn't even give him a chance to decide for himself. Maybe he thinks you're not interested in him."

"That couldn't be," Lisa protested.

"I'm not so sure," Molly said. "Adam and I spent a couple of years telling ourselves that the other one wouldn't be interested. Lisa, did I tell you that Adam said he'd tried to ask me out twice before but that I'd said no? I thought about it and I remembered two times when I thought he was just being sorry for me. I did say no, but I didn't understand the question."

Molly's smile was soft and sweet, and for the first time since she'd known her, Lisa thought of Molly as pretty. Of course she was not perfect in figure or feature, but she was lovable. Lisa could see that Molly was very, very happy, and she was glad for her. As for herself, Lisa was sure that Molly was wrong. "I know you're wrong," Lisa told her. "I just know it."

"Where would it hurt to let Rick know you're in love with him?" Molly asked softly.

"I couldn't do that," Lisa said quickly.

"Where would it hurt to let Rick know you'd like to date him again?"

"My pride," Lisa admitted. "It would hurt my pride."

"How about if I let him know?" Molly offered.

Lisa thought about that a long time. Then she said slowly, "Be careful what you say. Just sort of let him know that I'm not dating John exclusively. If Rick looks as though he couldn't care less, then let it drop."

"You want me to walk up to him and say, Lisa Kelly doesn't just date fellows named John?"

Lisa laughed at the thought and amended, "You know what to say. Just don't lay it on too thick. I'm sure you're wrong, but I'll go along this far—hint. If he doesn't take the hint, drop it. Promise me?"

"I promise," Molly said seriously. "Now, run along

so I'll have a chance to talk with him for a minute or two before the shop closes."

"Go home early?" Lisa asked.

"Thirty minutes early won't hurt this one time," Molly said. "If Adam wants to know where you are, I'll say you have a dentist appointment."

"All right," Lisa said doubtfully. Mr. Brewster was a nice man but he was very fussy about everyone keeping regular hours. She didn't want to do anything to anger him. She wanted to keep her job on Saturdays during the next school year. In fact, she'd been thinking of asking if she could come in for a couple of hours each day after school to help with the cleanup. It was very important for her to appear responsible. But if Molly said it was all right, it would be all right, she told herself. Lisa went home quickly before she lost her nerve and begged Molly not to say anything.

Lisa was doing the supper dishes when the telephone rang. She dried her hands on a towel and picked up the receiver, expecting it to be for one of her parents or Eddie. She knew that John was at a barbecue that evening because she'd refused to go with him. When the voice on the other end asked, "Lisa?" it took her a few seconds to place whose voice it was.

"Rick?" she asked.

"Hi, Lisa. I thought maybe I'd come over, if that's all right with you. We could go for a drive or something." Rick's voice sounded shy.

"Fine," Lisa said. Then she amended quickly, saying, "I mean, I'd love to, but I can't go out. I'm baby-sitting my brother Eddie."

"We could just sit in the car and talk," Rick said.

Lisa knew her parents would have a fit if they came

home and found her sitting in front of the house with some boy in a car. She said, "We could sit on the porch. Eddie will be watching television."

"Good," Rick said. "I'll be there in ten minutes."

Lisa raced up to her room and changed from her old yellow shirt to a clean and bright lavender one. She barely had time to let her long black hair down from the topknot on top of her head before Rick rang the bell.

Lisa was so nervous her teeth were chattering as she said, "Hi, Rick. Do you want a Coke or anything?"

"Not for a minute," he said. "I'm too nervous. Look, I want to talk to you, O.K?"

Lisa's heart was beating so loudly that she thought he might hear it as she followed him out and sat down beside him on the white porch swing at the side of their house. He said, "This is a great swing. Do you sit here a lot?"

"Sometimes," Lisa said. "But this summer has been so hot that I've stayed inside a lot. That is, most of the time, I've been working . . ." Her voice trailed off and she prayed that she wouldn't fall into the dreadful silence again.

"I wanted to talk to you before," Rick began. "But you seemed sort of . . . sort of unfriendly."

"No," Lisa said. "I didn't feel unfriendly. I just wanted you to be . . . free . . . . I mean . . ." Again, she ran out of words. But this time she wasn't as depressed as she had been. Maybe Molly was right. Maybe she'd been too quick to assume that Rick wasn't interested in her. Maybe the fact that he was sitting beside her on the porch right now showed that he did have some little interest in her, after all.

"I wanted to ask you out again," Rick said. "I

thought we had a good time. But you said you just wanted to be friends. I thought that meant you didn't want to go out with me again."

Lisa smiled at Rick and shook her head. "I thought you didn't want to go out with me again."

Rick's brown eyes seemed to be almost black in the early-evening light. He was smiling as he said, "I thought that you thought but all the time you thought that I thought."

Lisa and Rick laughed together. They both began talking at the same time, "Then you really would like . . ." This time they both stopped talking and laughed loudly.

Rick took Lisa's hand and said, "What about tomorrow night? What's doing with you?"

"Nothing," Lisa said. That wasn't really true. She'd promised John that she would go bowling with him, but she could break the date.

"Would you like to drive out to the lake with me? We could swim and then get a hamburger. Maybe even dance if the jukebox is working," Rick asked.

Lisa nodded her head. "I'd love to."

"You should see your eyes in this light," Rick said. "They look like those pansies over there." He pointed to the wooden window box of purple pansies and red geraniums fastened to the porch railing. Then he leaned forward and kissed her lips.

Lisa slipped her arms around Rick's shoulders and pressed her lips to his. It was a beautiful feeling to be sitting with the fellow she loved, kissing him, and she wanted the moment to last forever. When Rick drew away, it was all Lisa could do not to hold on to him.

He put his hands on her shoulders and whispered, "You're beautiful, Lisa. You look beautiful in the moonlight." Then he kissed her lightly and stood up to go.

Lisa stood beside him, leaned forward and kissed him again. Then she laughed and said, "Do you know this is the first time I've kissed you standing up? I wondered how it would work."

When he looked puzzled, she explained. "I'm so tall. I didn't see how it would work."

He kissed her again, holding her close to him for a minute, and then said, "Works very well, doesn't it?"

Lisa leaned her head against his shoulder and whispered, "Yes. Yes, it does."

As she watched Rick leave the porch and walk down the sidewalk to his truck, some of the old worries came back to her. She couldn't help but wonder how much of Rick's interest in her was because of her and how much was because Patty was out of town. Lisa frowned slightly at the August moon and promised herself that she wouldn't worry about that tonight. Even if Rick did lose interest in her when Patty came home, it would be worth it. Five weeks dating Rick would be better than a year with someone like John.

At the thought of John, Lisa's frown deepened. She went into the house and called him on the telephone, making an excuse to break the date tomorrow night. John sounded disappointed but he didn't argue or complain. He did ask, "How about the next night?"

"I'll be busy for a few nights," Lisa lied.

"I'll call you Friday," John said.

Lisa hesitated. Should she tell John the truth? Was it fair to him to keep him on the string now that she was dating Rick? But how could she be sure that Rick would ask her out again? One date—one kiss—wasn't the same thing as going steady. No. She didn't want to discourage John completely. "Call me on Sunday," Lisa suggested.

But by Sunday, Lisa was more in love with Rick than ever. What's more, Rick seemed very interested in her. He'd asked her out three times that week. Once they'd gone to the movies, and twice they'd gone to the lake swimming. Lisa was wonderfully, deliriously happy as she told John, "I'm sorry, but I just am way too busy right now."

"You're dating Rick Brewster," John said. There was a dull, sad ring to his voice.

Lisa felt herself getting angry with John. It was almost as though he were accusing her of something evil. She said, "We never agreed to go steady. It's true that I'm dating Rick, but there's no need for you to sound so angry. You date other people."

"It's not the same," John accused.

"It's the same," Lisa argued. "A date is a date."

"But I only date other people when you say no," John pointed out.

Lisa didn't know what else to say. In a way, she hoped that John would get so mad that he would hang up the telephone and never call her again. In another way, she hated to make anyone unhappy, especially someone who had been as nice to her as John had. After all, it was John who had first told her she was beautiful. It was John who had been so good to her and taken her so many nice places. If John hadn't been around these last few months, she didn't know what she would have done. Finally, she said, "Look, John, I am dating Rick. But that doesn't mean I don't like you. It just means I'm busy right now."

"But if you like me, you can go out with me too," John said reasonably.

Lisa sighed. "All right. We could go to the movies this Friday night. O.K.?" She knew that Rick was going with his father to some kind of Boy Scout dinner for his brother. It would be safe to go out with John then.

John seemed satisfied with her promise to date him that next Friday. When he hung up the telephone, Lisa forgot him almost immediately. These days her head was full of Rick and all the wonderful things that Rick had said to her. Lisa smiled dreamily at the telephone and twirled around in happiness. Yes—dating Rick was just as glorious as she'd always dreamed. Then she ran upstairs to get her white shawl. She and Rick were driving out to the Riverside Café to have a Coke tonight.

The moon was a small sliver as they drove down the dark country road that night. Lisa leaned against Rick's shoulder and looked up at it. She said, "I made a wish on that moon two weeks ago. And guess what happened?"

"Your wish came true?"

Lisa let her laughter float out over the silver lake. She felt so deliriously happy to be sitting beside Rick, to be leaning on his shoulder, to feel so close to him. She wished that the moment could go on forever. Even as she thought it, the knowledge that her summer romance would soon come to a close hit her like a sharp stab of fear. She shivered and Rick dropped his arm around her shoulder, asking, "Cold?"

She wanted with all her heart to tell Rick what she'd been thinking. She would have liked to ask him how he really felt about her. But she didn't dare bring the thought of Patty into Rick's mind. She said, "I'm a little cold. But we're almost there."

"Funny how hot it was two weeks ago," Rick said. "Now it almost feels as though fall is coming."

Lisa felt the tears burn her eyes. Was that a hint of hope in Rick's voice when he spoke of fall? Was he missing Patty that much? Would he forget all about Lisa when the slim, blond girl came back into his life?

"You're not laughing," Rick said. "You're usually laughing. That's one of the things I like about you, Lisa. You always seem to see the bright side of things."

"So do you," Lisa said. "You're always cheerful."

He pulled her closer to him and said, "Especially since I met you. You're my girl, Lisa. O.K.?"

"O.K." Lisa's voice caught as she gave the simple answer. What did Rick mean when he called her his girl? Was it only a simple expression of affection, or did it mean that he was really serious about her? She didn't know and she didn't dare ask.

Once they were inside the café, Lisa brought the subject back to the easiest and safest thing they could talk about: work. She asked, "Do you think your dad and Molly are serious about each other?"

"Yes. Dad asked me yesterday how I'd like a step-mother."

"And what did you say?"

"I said I wouldn't think of having a stepmother unless she happened to be Molly. That Molly would be all right, but anyone else was out of the question." Rick was smiling and his eyes seemed filled with happiness as he said, "Everyone's in love this summer."

"Everyone?" Lisa asked timidly.

"My dad and Molly, you and me, my little brother and some kid named Charlie; even my cat has a girlfriend," Rick said in a light voice.

"Charlie?" Lisa asked. She tried to keep her tone as light as Rick's. Was he serious when he used the word love, or was it only conversation?

"Her real name is Charlene Louise O'Brien," Rick said.

As they were laughing, some kids from school came into the café and Rick called out to them. The rest of the evening was spent in a group, talking about the summer activities, the coming school year and the prospects for a decent football team. Lisa sat back, letting Rick do most of the talking and enjoying every minute of the evening. Over and over the last two weeks, she'd had to work at enjoying her good fortune. In the beginning she'd been nervous and ill at ease a lot of the time when they were with other kids. But gradually, she'd come to accept the fact that the others saw nothing remarkable about Rick Brewster dating Lisa Kelly. In fact, most of them seemed to take it as a natural consequence of working together. None ever mentioned Patty, and Lisa was grateful for that.

Lisa was grateful for a lot of things when she thought about it. She was grateful that she was feeling so much better about herself. She knew that this summer had been a special summer for her. She'd developed a lot more self-confidence. It was easier for her to make friends and talk with people than ever before. She was finding that a lot of people seemed to admire her easy humor and good nature. Once in a while, someone even said something to let her know that she looked pretty.

It was a wonderful feeling to be sitting beside Rick, to have him put his hand on her arm as though to claim her. Lisa felt a small thrill each time someone asked questions that made them a couple. Tom asked, "You two going to the Grange picnic tomorrow night?"

"I don't know," Rick answered. Then he turned to Lisa and smiled that wonderful warm smile as he asked in a slow, loving voice, "What do you say we go?"

"Fine," Lisa answered. And she felt warm and good all over. It was a small moment but just one more token of how much Rick included her in his life. For Rick seemed very steady and sure about having Lisa around as much as possible.

Finally, Rick stretched and yawned and said, "Time to go. Lisa and I have to work tomorrow."

"That must be weird," Mary Lou said. "I mean, it must be weird to work for your boyfriend."

Rick's laughter was loud and long. "I'm not her boss. She's *my* boss. You should see her in action. I've never worked as hard in my life as I have since Lisa's been there."

The next morning, Lisa reminded him of his statement the minute she saw him. She smiled a great, happy smile and said, "O.K., Rick. Get to work. I'm the boss, so I'll just supervise."

Rick reached up and put his arm around her shoulder, pulling her toward him as though he were going to fight with her. She laughed and pulled away. He reached forward again and would have grabbed her, but his father roared from the office, "Rick! Cut the kidding and get to work."

Lisa blushed and so did Rick. She knew that Mr. Brewster often thought that Rick didn't take his work seriously enough and she was sorry he'd seen their little game. It wasn't as though she and Rick wasted time on the job. They really worked hard when they worked together, but Lisa knew that Adam Brewster would never believe that now.

Her face was still flushed when Molly came back from the post office and said, "Lisa, you'd better go with Rick to pick up the geraniums from Albert's Farm. Mike isn't here and it will take Rick all day to load that truck by himself."

"Are you sure?" Lisa asked. "Did Mr. Brewster say it was all right?"

Molly laughed. "I'm the boss around here, you know. He didn't hire me as manager so I'd ask every little thing. Don't worry, and have a good time. You can stop for lunch if you want. By the time you get the truck loaded and back here, it will be noon anyway."

Lisa grabbed her jacket and went out the side door before Mr. Brewster could call her back. She had an idea he wouldn't approve of sending her along to help Rick, but she tried not to worry about that. It was Molly's job to worry, not hers.

Rick seemed to be just as delighted as she was about having her along as an assistant. He talked all the way to Albert's Farm, pointing out the sights along the way. It was the first time Lisa had ever ridden with Rick during working hours and she thought it was fun. Unlike Rick, who liked working outdoors more than in the shop, Lisa didn't want to ride in the truck all day. She still loved working with flowers as much as ever and dreamed of becoming an artistic designer of floral arrangements for some large florist someday. If she couldn't do that, she hoped to work in a greenhouse and florist shop the way Molly did.

Rick told her about the farmhouse they were pulling up to as he turned the truck so that the bed faced a long shed to the right of the house. "This farm has been in Albert's family for two hundred years. Albert's over seventy now and very proud of the place. He breeds sheep and grows geraniums because that's what he likes. It's a good life."

Just then, Albert came out of the shed, waving his arm and warning Rick, "Don't get too close. Don't dent my shed."

Rick killed the motor and jumped out of the truck. Lisa followed him quickly. Albert, who was very bent, leaned on a stick and looked up at Lisa. He whistled between his teeth and said to Rick, "You got yourself a tall girlfriend, didn't you?"

"Lisa Kelly, meet Albert Somerville. Lisa works at the shop with me."

"Can't kid me, she's your girlfriend," Albert said. Then he turned and walked back into the shed, saying, "They're all ready to go."

Lisa and Rick carried boxes of small geranium cuttings from the shed to the truck. There were four hundred boxes of geraniums and they stacked them carefully, one of top of the other along the walls of the truck. "These are an experiment," Rick told her. "My dad thinks we can sell geraniums year round, so we're trying cuttings that will bloom about Christmas time."

"I never thought of geraniums at Christmas," Lisa said. "Only poinsettias."

"Yes, but geraniums are red, too. And cheaper. It's an idea that Molly and my dad argued about one evening for two hours. Molly is sure he's crazy, but my dad thinks he's right. He's got his heart on selling hundreds of geraniums this Christmas."

Lisa wasn't sure whether the geranium idea was a

good or a bad one, but she did love the little cuttings. Ever since she'd found that geraniums could be reproduced just by cutting off a stem and sticking it into loose soil, she'd been enchanted by the plants. It had seemed like magic when she'd first learned of it and it still seemed like magic to her.

She bent over one box, poked her finger into the loose soil, straightening one small cutting, and said, "They're so cute."

"So are you," Rick said. He was behind her in the truck and he grabbed her around the waist, turning her so that she faced him. Rick kissed her quickly and she pulled back, protesting, "Rick, Albert will see!"

"So what?" Rick asked. "He already knows you're my girl." But he let her go and they both hopped out of the back of the panel truck onto the ground.

"I wonder how he knew," Lisa mused.

"Because you're so pretty," Rick answered promptly. "He knew I wouldn't let you go without a fight." Then he laughed and teased, "Also, he knows all the women are crazy about me."

As Rick turned to take the invoice slips to Albert, Lisa felt that old sharp stab of fear in the pit of her stomach. It was true. A lot of girls were crazy about Rick. Would she be able to keep him after school started and Patty came back? As school drew closer and closer, Lisa felt more and more discouraged about her chances.

While they drove back toward Wilmington, Lisa tried to concentrate on the beautiful bright fields. August was one of the prettiest months in New England, and she loved looking at the green trees and brighter green fields. Often, they passed small farmhouses with bright red rosebushes climbing along the rock walls or over trellis slats. As always, Lisa exclaimed at the beauty of the flowering shrubs and grasses.

Rick suggested they get some hamburgers at McDonald's and have a picnic. They made their selections and drove out into a large flat meadow. When they parked, Lisa said, "Let's eat outside."

"No place to sit," Rick said. "No blanket, and the ground is rocky and full of stickers."

"We could sit in the back," Lisa suggested. "That way, we could look out at the mountains."

Rick agreed cheerfully and they walked around to the back of the truck. He opened the doors and they jumped up onto the bed of the truck. There wasn't much room because the boxes of geraniums lined both walls, but Lisa and Rick squirmed in happily. Their legs hung over the edge as they ate their hamburgers and drank their Cokes. They watched the clouds chase one another across the sky and chattered happily about nothing in particular.

Suddenly, a dark cloud seemed to come from nowhere and race across the sky, chasing all the little white ones away. Lisa shivered and said, "It's getting cold. I think it's going to rain."

"You just want me to put my arm around you," Rick teased. "But I'm too busy eating french fries."

Lisa laughed and said, "Conceited thing! But you're wrong. Look, it's raining."

The sky seemed to open up and pour buckets of black water down on them. Lisa looked down at her legs sticking out of the truck and said, "I'm getting soaked. We'd better get back into the cab."

"Nope," Rick said, "We're entitled to a thirty-minute lunch break. Let's close the door and sit in the back."

"What for?" Lisa asked.

Rick laughed and said, "I'm finished with the french fries. I thought I'd put my arm around you now."

Before Lisa really knew what was happening, Rick had pulled her inside the truck and was pulling the doors closed. She said, "Don't do that, Rick."

He stopped, looked at her seriously for a moment and then said, "Lisa, you don't have to worry when you're with me. I wouldn't do anything to hurt you."

Lisa felt her face flush and she said, "I know that, Rick. But I wouldn't feel right with the doors closed. O.K.?"

"O.K.," he agreed and pulled her close to him. They were inside the truck now, sitting with their legs stretched out in front of them and their backs against a tall row of geranium flats. Lisa leaned her head against Rick's shoulder and said, "Listen to it rain. It sounds wonderful on that tin roof."

"It's saying, 'Beautiful Lisa, beautiful Lisa,' " Rick said. "Can you hear it?"

Lisa listened seriously for a moment. The rain was making a sort of rhythmic pattern that could be something like "beautiful Lisa." She said, "How do you know it isn't saying, 'Handsome Rick'?"

"Nothing doing," Rick said. "Listen to the beat. Iambic pentameter for sure. Da-da-di di-da."

Lisa laughed and pretended to push Rick away from her. "That's not iambic pentameter and you know it."

Rick turned and brought his face close to hers, leaning forward to kiss her. His voice was low and soft as he said, "Actually, I wouldn't know it. I flunked the poetry unit."

Lisa reached up and pulled Rick's face down on hers. She didn't want to talk anymore. She wanted to be as close to Rick as she could be. She wanted to touch him, to love him, to kiss him.

Rick said in a rough voice, "Lisa, beautiful Lisa," and pulled her close to him to kiss her. It was the strongest, roughest and most exciting kiss they'd ever shared. Lisa felt her heart beating very fast as she responded to Rick's embrace. For a few moments, she seemed to be all feeling, all sensension. There was no more worry about the future, no more fear of losing Rick. For a moment it was enough to be here beside him, to be close to him, to be with him.

She never knew exactly what happened after that. One moment she was kissing Rick, holding him tight, and the next moment a whole stack of geranium flats came crashing down on them. She supposed that she or Rick must have shifted suddenly, but she would never be sure. All she knew was that one moment she was blissfully happy and the next minute she was scrambling, trying to dig herself and Rick out from under mounds of dirt and boxes.

Rick's eye was cut and Lisa was screaming as she pulled him over to the doorway. Then she reached out into the cold summer air, cupped her hand and pulled in some water to wash the cut. The water she held in her hand dripped onto the floor of the truck, making mud of the geranium dirt. Rick said, "Don't, Lisa. You're making a mess. We'll never get this straightened out now."

"But you're hurt," Lisa said. She was frightened and almost crying.

"Never mind," he said shortly. "Just help me get the mess straightened out."

Lisa insisted, "Take off your T-shirt. I'll use that to wash your cut. You're bleeding."

Rick stripped off his T-shirt and Lisa held it out into the rain. Soon she had a corner of it wet enough to wipe away the blood. The wound was a surface one, and she could see that Rick wasn't really too hurt. That was when she agreed to stop worrying about him and start worrying about putting some order into the mess in front of her.

Two hours later, Lisa and Rick drove in to Brewster Florist. Rick's head was bandaged with a strip from the wet T-shirt and they were both covered with mud. Worst of all, they'd only been able to salvage half of the geranium flats. There was no way they could cover up their error.

Rick looked very grim as he pulled into the yard. Lisa said, "You can tell your dad it was my idea to have a picnic in the bed of the truck. Maybe that will help."

"Nothing will help," Rick said. "He's going to be furious with me, so that's that."

Lisa felt awful as she stood beside Rick while he explained to Mr. Brewster. Rick told the truth, leaving out the part about kissing Lisa, but Lisa was sure by the way Mr. Brewster looked that he knew they were necking in the truck. She only hoped he didn't think it was more serious than it really was. She couldn't stand to have Mr. Brewster think that.

As Rick talked, his father got redder and redder in the face. Lisa finally began to worry about his blood pressure. She thought that for the first time in her life she understood the expression about being so angry you could explode. Mr. Brewster did look as though he might explode, and Lisa worried about him as well as Rick and herself.

Finally, Rick finished, saying, "So, you see, it really was an accident. I'll go back to Albert's tomorrow and see if he has more geraniums. I'll pay for them myself."

"You sure will!" Mr. Brewster said. "Of all the irresponsible stories I've ever heard, that's the worst! I'll tell you the truth, if you weren't my son, I'd fire you. But you can't fire your own kids, so you'll pay for the geraniums. And you'll stay in for a week. Silly, girl-crazy kid. I don't know . . ." He broke off and said, "Get home and get cleaned up. Then go to the doctor and see if you can get stitches in that. So stupid you didn't even know enough to get a cut stitched up! Go on, get out of here!"

Rick turned to go without another word. Lisa could tell by the way his jaw was so tight that he was almost as angry as his father was. For the first time, she saw how much they were alike. But she wasn't worried about Rick at the moment; she was worried about what Mr. Brewster would say to her. She waited, holding her breath, for him to start in on her.

He turned and went toward his office. In a small voice, Lisa asked, "What about me?"

Mr. Brewster turned and looked at her. She felt absolutely awful standing there, still wet and muddy and fighting back tears. All he said was, "You too. Get home." Then he turned his back on her.

By the way he slammed the door she could tell he was really very, very angry. She didn't dare ask him if she was fired. She didn't dare ask anything at all. Lisa turned and went out the door of Brewster Florist.

Rick was waiting for her outside the door. He took her hand and said softly, "So now you know about the Brewster temper. Pretty awful, isn't it?"

"You didn't lose your temper," Lisa reminded him.

"I was wrong," Rick said simply.

Lisa's heart seemed to grow and blossom as she looked at the fine young man beside her. He was really just as wonderful as she'd dreamed. At first, she'd thought of him as a kind of cardboard hero, but now that she really knew him, she truly admired him. She wanted to tell him how much he meant to her but she couldn't find the right words.

Finally, she said, "I guess our date is off for tonight?"

"Yes. He'll stay mad for a couple of days. I'll be on restriction for the whole week. My dad is fair but he doesn't back down."

"I'm sorry," Lisa said.

"So am I," Rick said. "Not sorry my dad is fair, but sorry it happened. But it's not the end of the world, Lisa. A week isn't so long, you know." They were at the corner where they should part to go their different ways. Rick kissed her on the cheek and grinned, trying his hardest to look lighthearted as he said, "The kiss was worth the trouble, my darling."

Lisa smiled, batting back the tears with her long black eyelashes. She said softly, "You really are a wonderful person, Rick. You're good and kind and sweet."

". . . and a gentleman," Rick added in a laughing voice, but Lisa was sure that her praise had pleased him. She was glad that she'd been able to say something to make him feel a little better.

14

Lisa waited anxiously for Rick to call her that evening. She wasn't sure whether or not she'd been fired from Brewster Florist and she didn't want to go in to work the next morning if she had been. Mr. Brewster had looked very angry, but she didn't think he had actually fired her. At least she hoped not.

When ten o'clock came and Rick hadn't phoned, Lisa went up to bed. It had been a full day and she was tired. Even so, she didn't fall right asleep but spent a while going over the day's events in her mind. Certainly the ending with Rick's father had been dreadful, but there had been good parts too. As she drifted off to sleep, she imagined she could still feel Rick's arms around her and still feel his lips on her lips.

Her dreams were not of Rick, though, but of Patty Baker. Lisa woke at four in the morning with Patty's taunts still in her ears. In the night, Patty had come to her and warned her that she would be coming home in two and a half weeks. She'd said, "I'll have him back, you know. He's mine," and then Lisa had awakened.

She tossed and turned but never really did get back to sleep. When it was time to get up, she went to the mirror and was startled to see dark circles under her eyes. She'd never thought about teenagers getting circles or bags. It didn't seem fair; teenagers had so many other problems, like bad skin. Not that her own skin was ever anything but clear, Lisa thought as she scrubbed her face. Later, she applied a little makeup to cover the circles and lipstick to make her face look more cheerful. When she finished, she brushed her long black hair into a ponytail and tied it with a lavender ribbon.

She put on her lavender blouse, thinking that if she were to be fired, she would at least look good during her last appearance. Turning to look in the mirror one last time, Lisa smiled at her reflection. Yes. Even she could see that this summer had changed her for the better. Rick said she was beautiful. So did John. Well, even if she still couldn't see that, she could see that she was better looking. Her figure was fuller, rounder, and she was standing up straighter. She knew that she'd finally become reconciled to her height. Five feet ten and a half wasn't the tallest woman in the world, and she had definitely stopped growing. There were even some advantages to being tall. She could see in crowds. She could wear beautiful clothes like her prom dress. It had helped her get the job at the florist shop.

At the thought of Brewster Florist, Lisa's mood fell. She took a deep breath, practiced smiling once again and went out the door to go to work. She wasn't sure whether or not she really had work, but there was no way to find out except to go in.

Molly was friendly. She looked up from her work, grinned and said, "Hear you and your boyfriend had a little trouble yesterday."

"Am I fired?" Lisa asked.

Molly shook her head quickly and said, "Of course not. Adam went out for doughnuts. He'll be in soon and he's still upset, so get to work."

"Is Rick here?"

Molly made a face. "He's going to be working in Lenox all week. I think it's part of his punishment. Adam was going to have Mike do it, but now Rick is stuck."

Thinking of how Rick hated to work inside all the time, Lisa felt very sorry for him. But she felt even sorrier for herself because that meant that she wouldn't be able to see Rick at work or in the evenings. Lisa sighed and bent over to cut the first cord on the first box of flowers. She knew there was no sense crying over spilled milk. What's done was done and there was no going backward, but she did think it was too terrible that there was so little time left and she wouldn't be able to spend it all with Rick. Sometimes life was very hard.

She was working so fast when Mr. Brewster came in that she didn't hear him until he said, "Not going to have a doughnut today, Lisa? Where's that famous appetite?"

Lisa stood up, put her hands on her hips and stretched. She smiled at Adam Brewster in appreciation of his friendliness and said, "I'd like a doughnut."

Later that day, Lisa tried to apologize for what had

happened in the truck. She and Mr. Brewster were working together, stacking some empty plastic pots along one wall of the shed beside the greenhouse. It was hard, dirty work, and Lisa knew that if Rick were there, he and not his father would be helping her.

Adam Brewster must have been thinking the same thing, because he grunted and groaned every time he bent to lift another stack of pots. He said, "This is no work for old men. If that darn kid of mine weren't so worthless, he'd be doing this."

Lisa wanted to tell Mr. Brewster that it wasn't Rick's fault he wasn't helping. It was Mr. Brewster who had sent him to Lenox. Instead, she said, "I am sorry about yesterday, Mr. Brewster."

"It wasn't your fault," Mr. Brewster answered shortly.

"But if was half my fault," Lisa said. "In fact, it was more than half."

"Rick wasn't doing his job," he answered quickly. "It was Rick's fault."

"It was my idea to have a picnic inside the truck," Lisa insisted.

Mr. Brewster made a funny sound, then put his arm around Lisa's shoulder. He said, "Lisa, you're a good girl. You're a good worker and a sweet person. The minute I saw you, I thought, now there's a sweet girl. Not like some of the girls that girl-crazy son of mine has dated. I won't say any more . . . but believe me, you're not the first girl that Rick has made a fool of himself over. At least you're a sweetheart, but that's not the point. The point is, Rick was in charge of that truck. It was his responsibility and he messed up. You're not to blame, he is. Now let's get back to the store, or Molly will think I'm picking on you again. She really let me have it for scaring her best hired help. I guess I do have quite a temper."

Lisa followed docilely behind Mr. Brewster. She was sorry she hadn't been able to convince Mr. Brewster that part of the blame was hers, but she was relieved that he seemed so sure she was a nice girl. It had bothered her a lot that he might think anything different.

Later in the day, when she was thinking of their conversation, it occurred to her that Mr. Brewster probably didn't like Patty very well. She knew he'd been very angry on the day Molly sprained her ankle because Rick and Patty were gone. That time it hadn't really been Rick's fault either. As far as Lisa could see, Mr. Brewster had very high standards for his son. Still, Rick didn't seem to think his dad was unfair and he was a happy person. Maybe high standards made good sons, Lisa told herself.

As she thought over the conversation she found herself worrying more than ever about Patty's return. Mr. Brewster had hinted that Rick had been just crazy about Patty. Was Rick still really more interested in Patty than in her? Lisa shook her head to clear the worry from her brain and began sweeping the store for the final cleanup.

As she swept she tried to remember some of the good things she and Rick had done together that summer. At least she would always have those memories, she told herself. But no matter how hard she tried, she couldn't get the nagging fear from her mind. As she had many times before, Lisa told herself that it hurt to be in love.

The telephone rang and Lisa answered it. It was

Rick's little brother, who asked for Rick. "He's not here," Lisa said.

"He's on his way," the boy said. "I called the Lenox store and they said he was on his way there. So tell him he's got a letter from his girlfriend."

"His girlfriend?" Lisa asked stupidly.

"Patty finally wrote him," the boy explained. "I know he's been waiting for the letter, so I called to tell him. Will you tell him?"

"If I see him," Lisa promised. As she hung up the telephone, her fingers felt numb. So Rick was waiting for a letter from Patty, and now it was there. All along, while he'd been dating her, Rick had been writing to Patty. Lisa didn't trust herself to say or do the right thing when Rick came into the shop. Instead of waiting to see him, she went to Molly and asked, "All right if I go home a little early? I feel kind of sick."

"Sure," Molly answered. "You look sort of pale. Anything serious?"

"I don't know," Lisa said. "I just don't know."

15

Rick called her that evening, explaining that his father had forbidden him to contact her before this. He said quietly over the telephone, "I miss you."

"I miss you too," Lisa answered. She wanted to ask about his letter from Patty but she didn't dare. All that summer, they'd never once mentioned Patty or Rick's relationship to her. It was almost as though the blond girl didn't exist. Yet Lisa knew that Patty was very much alive and would be returning soon. It was for that reason she had promised John she'd go out with him again.

Now, as she was talking to Rick, she was very much aware that she was going to the movies with John tomorrow night. A sharp thought crossed Lisa's mind. What if Rick's father let him off restriction? What would she do then? It wouldn't be fair to break another date with John, and she certainly hadn't ever agreed with Rick not to date anyone else. That was another of those subjects, like Patty, that just hadn't come up. Rick must know that she wasn't seeing much of John because she was seeing so much of him, but he never asked.

Rick didn't ask many questions, she realized as they chatted on the telephone. She had an idea that he thought it wasn't good manners. He was really a very polite person and sensitive to other people's feelings. Now, as she talked with him, she wished with all her heart that she could be with him. It would be wonderful to be walking beside him, holding his hand, kissing him again. But telephone conversations were better than nothing, so she enjoyed their talk together. When he got ready to say good night, he said, "I'm off restriction next Monday. That's your day off. How about if I get the day off too and we go to the lake for the day? Get in the last rays of summer?"

"Love it," Lisa said quickly, though any reference to the end of summer made her nervous. Then she said casually, "I thought I'd go to the movies tomorrow night."

"You stinker!" Rick cried in mock pain. "Just don't see the new Woody Allen movie. That's for us."

"I won't go if you don't want me to," Lisa offered. She felt just awful about having a date with another fellow while Rick was stuck in the house.

"It's O.K.," Rick said. "I was just kidding. Besides, I'm catching up on my television. I'll be able to tell you the plots of every old western on TV."

Lisa was still feeling guilty when John picked her up for the movies the next night. She couldn't help comparing him all evening to Rick. He seemed more nervous and more pathetically eager to please her than ever. Her reaction was the same mixture of anger at him for being such a persistent follower and guilt about mistreating someone who'd never done her any harm.

The worst part of the evening was when he took her home and tried to kiss her good night. She just didn't feel like being kissed by anyone but Rick. She leaned away and said, "Please don't, John. I'm not in the mood."

"You're never in the mood anymore," John said.

It irritated her when John's voice sounded that way. To Lisa, that particular tone of voice always reminded her of her little brother Eddie when he was being his most obnoxious. She said, "John, I don't have to kiss anyone I don't want to."

"No, of course not," John said quickly.

This time she was irritated because he agreed so quickly. Why did John have to be so nice and why did his niceness have to make her so mad? She asked sharply, "Are you dating other people?"

"No . . . I mean yes. What do you want me to say?" John asked.

"I just think you should date other people. It isn't right just to hang around me." Lisa knew she sounded very cross.

John's face crumpled, and for a minute Lisa thought he was going to cry. He asked softly, "Does that mean you don't ever want to go out with me again?"

"Oh, I don't know what it means," Lisa said. Suddenly, she felt his fear and understood that it was a lot like her own fear. John feared he'd never see her again, and she feared she'd never see Rick again. It was a terrible circle of fear, and everyone seemed trapped in it. She felt very sorry for John and, impulsively, leaned over and kissed him.

John smiled at her gratefully and asked, "Can I call you again?"

"Call me in a week," Lisa said. Then she slipped out of the car and went into the house. Once inside, she was furious with herself for not telling John she didn't want to see him anymore. There just didn't seem to be any point to continuing the sad phone calls and occasional dates. It wasn't making John any happier and it was making her feel awful. Besides, she didn't know whether Rick wanted her to date anyone else or not. Lisa sighed and poured herself a glass of milk. That was the center of the problem, wasn't it? She really didn't know what was going on with Rick, and until she knew that for sure, she didn't know what she wanted to do about John. In her heart, Lisa knew that she was holding to John because John was better than no one—and when Patty came home, she might have no one.

But if Lisa's thoughts were often on Patty, there was no sign that Rick's were. At work, he seemed to have no thoughts of anyone but her. Though he spent most of that long week in the Lenox store, he often came in for an hour or so in the afternoon to help Lisa clean up. As the days passed he would say, "Three more days," then "Two more days," then "Tomorrow and it's all over."

Finally, Monday came and Rick was off restriction. He picked Lisa up at nine thirty and she was ready for the day in the sun. She'd spent the night before making deviled eggs and a chocolate cake for their picnic. As she handed him the picnic hamper he laughed and asked, "What's this? Did you invite an army?"

"I eat a lot," Lisa said. "So do you."

"That's true," Rick said and kissed her lightly on the

cheek. "It's one of the reasons we make such a lovely couple. Right?"

"Right." She ran out to the panel truck and laughed aloud at the thought of their last adventure in it. Turning to Rick, she asked, "No geraniums?"

Rick shook his head. "Nothing but man-eating tigers and giant boa constrictors today. You'll be perfectly safe with me."

The drive out to the beach was wonderful. Though it was late August, the sun was shining brightly and Lisa couldn't see one cloud in the sky. There were quite a few people on the beach, but Rick and Lisa found a quiet spot over beside a tall group of rocks where they would be away from the crowd. Lisa spread out the blanket, lay down on it and smiled up at the warm sun. She said, "I was born for a life of sunbathing, not working."

"Me too," Rick agreed. "But you don't want to get burned." He handed her a bottle of suntan lotion and said, "Put this on. You have that white skin."

"Irish skin," Lisa said. "I used to hate my light skin and dark hair. No one else has this kind of coloring."

"Yeah, look," Rick said and he put his dark brown arm against her whiter one. "I've got the brown hair and brown eyes, but you're a lot lighter." Then he traced his fingertips along her bare arm.

Lisa shivered, whether with the cool lake breeze she wasn't sure. When Rick drew his hand away, she rolled over on her stomach and asked, "Will you put some lotion on my back?"

It felt wonderful to have Rick's warm hand rub her back with lotion, and Lisa felt happy and carefree as she listened to the birds overhead. In the distance, she could hear the sound of motorboats and children laughing. She promised herself that she would be happy this day, that this would be a day to remember for always.

They lay in the sun for an hour and then went swimming. Lisa loved the feel of the cool lake water against her slightly burned skin. As she swam out, away from the edge of the land, she felt young and strong and brave enough to swim forever. Finally, she turned around, turned onto her back and faced the sun. Swimming on her back, she headed toward land. When she came in closer to shore, Rick was waiting for her. He laughed and said, "I'm hooked up with a mermaid. I had no idea you could swim like that."

Briefly, Lisa wondered if it bothered Rick that she could swim so well. Then she dismissed the thought. Rick was not that sort of person. He never made cracks about how girls were supposed to be weak or clinging. When they worked together in the shop, he never seemed to mind that she could lift and carry heavy things almost as easily as he could. No, Rick wasn't angry that she was a good swimmer. Rick was far too wonderful to worry about things like that.

They swam in to shore side by side, enjoying the feel of the water and pacing their strokes to stay together. When they were on land, Rick asked, "Want to take a walk?"

Lisa put her hand in his and said, "Sure."

She hoped they would walk away from the lake center, past their own rock and into the woods, but Rick chose to walk toward the crowd. He said, "I think I saw Larry and Tim earlier. Maybe they're here."

For the first time all day, a slight cloud entered Lisa's mood. She didn't really want to share this day with other people. Rick, who loved people, wouldn't understand those feelings, but she wanted more than anything to be alone with him. Nevertheless, she walked obediently by his side, and when she saw Tim's long, tall body standing beside the hot-dog stand, she pointed him out to Rick.

They followed Tim back to his blanket where Larry and Sally and John and Angela were sitting. Lisa was slightly embarrassed at the thought of having Rick and John meet each other. It wasn't as though she'd been deceiving either of them, she told herself, but she truly wasn't sure that Rick knew she was still dating John.

John turned pale and gulped when he said hello. Lisa could tell that he was very uncomfortable to see her there with Rick. She was sorry for him, but there wasn't much she could do. Poor John would just have to learn to take care of himself. She was a little surprised to see Angela sitting beside him. She wondered if they were together.

Rick dropped easily down on the blanket beside Tim and started a long conversation with him about the football team. Lisa stood on one foot, then the other, trying to keep her impatience from showing. She wished that Rick would finish his talk and they could go on their way. But Rick looked up and said, "Sit down, Lisa. There's plenty of room." He patted an empty spot beside him on the blanket.

Lisa dropped down beside Rick and turned to Angela. She said, "I haven't seen much of you this summer. You working?"

Angela nodded. "Baby-sitting for my cousin. It's kind of boring, but it was the best job I could get."

There was silence after that. Lisa felt uncomfortable trying to make conversation with Angela these days. They used to be such good friends and now they were just casual acquaintances. Lisa still had no idea what had happened between them, though she'd begun to suspect that it might have something to do with John. Again, she wondered exactly how often John and Angela went out together. And though she hated to admit it, she didn't like the idea of John having another girlfriend.

As in confirmation of her fears, she heard someone ask Rick, "When does Patty come home?"

"About a week," Rick said lightly.

Lisa waited for him to say something else, something like Lisa was his girl now, something comforting, but Rick only said, "I guess she had a good time in Colorado."

Unable to stand it any longer, Lisa turned to John and asked, "How about you? Have you had a good time this summer?" Then she smiled at him, letting him have the full force of her charm. If Rick was going to talk about Patty, then she might as well flirt with John. She would do anything to stop the dreadful feelings that were welling up inside her now.

John seemed taken aback by Lisa's sudden friendliness but he responded on cue. "I've had a good summer," he replied. "At least part of it has been good."

"Like August moon wishes and jazz concerts?" Lisa asked. She was referring to their two or three dates, trying desperately to draw John closer to her.

A look of surprised pleasure crossed John's face. His expression was the familiar one of admiration as he answered Lisa, "Yes, that was the best part."

Lisa scooped up a handful of sand and dribbled it slowly, carefully, over John's long legs as she said, "I enjoyed the jazz concert too. We should do it again."

For a minute John actually looked happy. She felt awful to be leading him on like this, but at the same time she felt good to know that she wouldn't be alone if . . . but that was too dreadful to think about. She leaned over and whispered, "We can do lots of things, John."

John blushed then and Lisa felt like laughing at him. Or crying. Why was he such a sap? By the same token, what did she think she was? She turned to see how Rick was taking her little flirtation with John.

But Rick was deep in the middle of a conversation with Tim and Mike about football and apparently hadn't even seen her demonstrate her power over John. She was disappointed and glad at the same time. In a way, she felt that John brought out the worst in her, and she disliked him for that. Though, to be honest, she knew that wasn't John's fault. It was her own.

Suddenly unable to bear another minute of the company, she rose and said, "Rick, I'm going to take a walk. I'll be back later."

He got to his knees and said, "I'll go with you."

"No. I'd just like to walk a little alone. Commune with nature, you know."

"Are you sure?" Rick asked. His face held an expression of confused concern. It was as though his eyes were asking if she was really all right.

"I'm sure," she said and forced herself to smile brightly. "I'll be back in about half an hour and then we can go eat lunch. O.K.?"

Lisa stood up and started walking along the lakeshore, picking her way between people on blankets and children playing on the sand. It was the first time she'd walked alone in a swimsuit all summer and she sensed a difference in the way people looked at her. Especially men.

Lisa knew the bright yellow two-piece swimsuit she was wearing was very pretty and she had an idea that it went well with her long black hair. But as she walked down the beach, she was surprised at how many people turned to stare at her. Once or twice she heard people say things about how good she looked and she was grateful for that. It helped her restore her confidence in herself.

She walked for a while, stopping to skip rocks across the water and pick up shells. Soon, her emotional balance was restored and she felt able to go back to Rick and the group of kids on the beach. She had used the time to talk to herself, to remind herself that she would be all right even if Rick did drop her when Patty came back. She was an attractive woman, she reminded herself, and no longer the skinny, awkward kid who'd fallen in love with Rick Brewster. She would never again be as shy and awkward as she'd been in the tenth grade.

As she walked back to the group she tried to make plans for next year. Maybe she would try to get active in something. Of course, she would still have the job at the flower shop and that would take up a lot of time. Lisa gulped at the idea of working in the flower shop while Rick was dating someone else; then she forced herself to stop worrying about a future she couldn't control. She would do the best she could, a day at a time, starting with this day.

Rick stood up when she walked toward the group they'd been talking to. "Let's eat," he said. "I'm starved."

"I thought you'd never ask." She laughed and held out her hand to him.

As Rick and Lisa walked away from the group, she heard someone say, "She's really great-looking, isn't she?"

Lisa sighed with pleasure. At least she wasn't kidding herself. She really had improved this summer. Even kids she'd known all her life were noticing the difference.

She turned to Rick and said, "First we eat, then we swim, then we run, then we . . ."

"Then we make out," Rick teased. "You don't think I brought you way out here in the wilderness for any purpose but romance, do you? I'm a very romantic fellow."

Lisa turned to him, laughing, and said, "You have to catch me first." Then she broke into a run toward the wonderful, clear lake water. It was good to be young. Good to be alive. Good to be in love.

16

Lisa came home from the lake burned, tired and happy. Deciding to live one day at a time had helped her through the rough spots and she'd been able to really enjoy most of the day.

She was surprised when her mother said that Angela had called and wanted her to call back. "Are you sure it was Angela?" Lisa asked, thinking her mother might just have assumed it was her old friend.

"Sure, I'm sure," her mother said. "She said to call as soon as you came in."

Lisa dialed Angela's number without looking it up in the book. During the ninth and tenth grade, they'd talked together nearly every day. She remembered the number well. She also remembered how much she'd enjoyed Angela's company in those days. Maybe Angela was ready to be friends again. At least Lisa hoped so.

"I'd like to come over and talk to you," Angela said when she picked up the telephone.

"It's late," Lisa answered. She didn't like the way Angela sounded and wanted to avoid whatever was coming.

"I'll be there in five minutes," Angela said and hung up.

Lisa waited on the porch for Angela, hugging her sweater to her. The sunburn made the August breeze seem cooler than it really was. Besides, she knew that Angela had been crying when she'd talked to her. She had an awful feeling that her old friend had something horrible to say to her. What could it be? She hoped that Angela wasn't in some terrible trouble.

She didn't have to wait long, because Angela was there in less than five minutes. When she came up the porch steps, she blurted out, "I just came to tell you that I hate you, Lisa Kelly."

"Hate me?" Lisa felt as though someone had knocked her in the stomach. "Why would you hate me?"

"You're just the most selfish, horrible girl I've ever known," Angela continued. "You don't care anything at all about John and you use him. He's a nice boy and you treat him like dirt."

Lisa took a deep breath, searching for words to defend herself. But could she explain to Angela how frightened she was of losing Rick? No. Angela was not her friend anymore. Angela would never understand. She said nothing.

"Ever since you got that job you've been stuck up and conceited and awful. You don't care about anyone but yourself and your beautiful body. You were just awful today. And I hate you!"

She's in love with John, Lisa thought. *That's why she's saying these awful things to me. It's because she's so in love with John that she can't help herself.* Out loud, Lisa said, "I did flirt with John today, and maybe I shouldn't have. But I didn't mean to hurt him. I can't help it if John is silly around me. That's not my fault."

"Yes, it is," Angela insisted stubbornly. "When he's not with you he's . . ."

". . . he's more interested in you," Lisa finished for her. "Look, Angie, I'm sorry. But you can't always make people love you. Even if John and I never saw each other again, I couldn't make him love you. Neither could you."

"I hate you!" Angela was screaming now. "You lead him on. You flirt with him. And all the time you've got Rick. You've got everything. You've got a good job, good looks, a nice boyfriend." Angela began to cry again. "I don't have anything and you've got it all."

Lisa put her arm around her old friend and said softly, "Look, Angie, I feel the same way you do sometimes. I don't really feel like I have anything, either. That's what made me flirt with John today. I was feeling just rotten because someone asked about Patty. The truth is, I'm scared to death that Rick will drop me when Patty comes back."

Angela drew back and wiped her eyes. She sniffed and asked, "You're not just telling me that to make me feel better?"

"No. It's the truth," Lisa said. Then she added, "I've missed you, Angela. And I'm sorry about John. You're probably right, you know. I do lead him on and I'm not interested in him." When she saw the look on Angela's face, she added quickly, "He's a nice fellow, and I can see why you like him. But we don't always have control over how we feel about people, do we?"

"No," Angela agreed. "I've had a crush on John for two years."

"You never told me," Lisa accused. "All that time you let me rave about Rick and you never even mentioned John." She was surprised that her old friend had kept secrets. Angela had always seemed so open and so careless about what she said. But people were full of surprises, weren't they? Right now, she was surprised at herself and how calmly she'd taken Angela's accusations.

As the girls talked, the tension seemed to disappear from the air. By the time Angela left, Lisa felt more comfortable with her than she had for a long time. She said to her old friend, "I don't know what I'll do about John for sure, but I promise you I won't lead him on anymore. I'll find some way to talk to him."

"Don't say anything about me," Angela begged.

"No," Lisa agreed solemnly. "It doesn't do any good to push anyone on people. All the time I was yearning for Rick, people kept telling me what a great fellow John was. It didn't do any good."

"It's all fate," Angela said, and then she yawned. "All that emotion made me tired. Good night."

Lisa called John the next day and asked him to come over. The conversation was brief, painful and blunt. She told him the truth. "I'm sorry I flirted with you the other day. I'm not interested in you. I don't know why, but it doesn't matter. I think it may be because we're too much alike. We're both quiet and shy. I need someone who's more outgoing."

"Someone like Rick?" John asked bitterly.

For once, Lisa refused to let herself be manipulated

into apologizing or changing her mind. "Yes, someone like Rick. Maybe not Rick, but someone like him. I'm sorry, John."

John seemed to sense a finality in her voice. He said, "O.K., Lisa. It was getting boring anyway, always waiting for you to give me a little attention. Maybe I'll look for a girl who's really interested in me."

Lisa wasn't upset that he was angry. Maybe his anger would make it easier for him to make a break. Maybe he would turn to Angela and they would be happy together. Whatever happened, Lisa knew that she was glad to have John out of her life. Even if it meant she would be alone.

At the thought of loneliness, her breath caught and she bit her lips to keep from calling John back. She was really frightened at the possibility that Rick would go back to Patty when she came home. It was only a week until she would know for sure. *Live one day at a time,* Lisa reminded herself and went back inside her house. This day, she was going to have fun.

The next week flashed by in a blur of work, fun and anxiety all rolled up into one. Lisa never found the nerve to mention Patty to Rick, and he didn't say anything about her imminent return until the day before Labor Day. Then he said, "Patty comes home tomorrow. I've promised to meet her at the airport. Her folks will expect it."

"All right," Lisa said.

"I have to talk to Patty, to give her a chance to get used to the idea that you and I are dating now. She didn't seem to understand my letters," Rick explained gently.

Lisa could hear a lot of anxiety in his voice as he told her that. She wondered what he'd written Patty and when. And why hadn't he told her before now? Most of all, she wondered how Rick would feel when he actually saw Patty get off that plane.

"I'll talk to Patty," Rick repeated. "Give her a chance to get used to the idea. It may take a while."

"When will I see you?" Lisa asked. She knew there was fear in her voice.

"I'll call you as soon as I can," Rick answered. "I don't want to embarrass her. You understand."

"Yes, I understand," Lisa said dully. She stared out the car window at the rainy night. Was this the last evening she'd ever be with Rick? Probably. But there was nothing she could do about that, she reminded herself. She couldn't make Rick love her. It was exactly the way she'd told Angela; no one could make anyone love another. Life was sad like that.

Lisa spent Labor Day in her room, pretending to have a cold. It was easier than attending the family picnic and pretending that everything was all right when it wasn't. Things wouldn't be all right until she heard from Rick again. Then she would be either happy or sad. If she were happy, that would be wonderful. If she were sad, she knew that she would have to make the effort to get over it. There were other boys in the world, other things to do besides wait for Rick Brewster. But on Labor Day, those thoughts were as faint as a distant pep talk for a stranger. As she lay with her face to the wall, letting the tears roll down her face, straining to hear the telephone ring, she could barely imagine an existence without Rick.

He didn't call on Labor Day. Nor did he call the next day. By the third day, Lisa was so miserable that she actually felt sick. She got out of bed in the morning, pulled on her Levi's and shirt, brushed her teeth and then went to the telephone to call in sick for the day. Tomorrow she would have to go back to work, but today she just couldn't face it. What would she say to Rick? How could she ever get through the day without breaking down? She was sure he would be sweet and sorry and try to explain things to her. Rick was always such a gentle person, but it wouldn't do any good. No matter how sweet Rick was about it, Lisa knew she would hate working with him now. She wondered if she should consider quitting her job.

The morning passed slowly. She lay on the couch looking at television until she couldn't stand it any longer. Then she made herself a glass of lemonade and went out to the porch to sit on the swing. As she rocked back and forth, her mind drifted back to that first night she'd sat here with Rick. That seemed a hundred years ago, though it was less than two months. How happy she'd been at the prospect of the long summer then. And how quickly the summer had flown away!

A butterfly fluttered in front of her. Lisa stopped the swing and looked at the beautiful yellow and brown wings as the butterfly hovered, then landed on the side of her swing. Lisa wanted to reach out and brush the velvet-soft wings, to feel the sweet comfort of touching another living thing. She felt so alone, so friendless and so sad. She reached out her hand, letting her fingers move slowly toward the lovely butterfly. It batted its wings and flew away. Lisa watched it until it disappeared, feeling very sorry for the loss of beauty.

She sat in the swing for a long time, thinking long and hard about her life and what she was going to do. In the end, she decided that she wouldn't quit her job. Losing

Rick wasn't the end of the world. She would go back to work tomorrow, listen to Rick's story and be as nice as he was. She could almost imagine her sweet smile as she said to him, "Those things happen, Rick. It was a good summer." Maybe, in time, they could become friends again. At least she hoped so, because she was sure of one thing—she really liked Rick Brewster a lot. She admired him as a person. In time, she hoped to admire herself as a person just as much. Right now, she felt that she had a little work to do.

No. She wasn't going to crumple into a whining ball just because Patty Baker was back in town. She was going to continue to feel like the attractive and interesting person she'd become this summer. Everything she'd learned about herself from Rick and John, she could remember. And she wouldn't go back to John, either. She was glad she'd cut John loose. Lisa kicked her legs out in front of her and sent the swing rocking back and forth. She would find some way to be happy without Rick. It would take time, but she would find a way. She wasn't going to be one of those girls who had to be in love to be alive. No, she wasn't.

The telephone rang and Lisa jumped out of the swing like a shot, running to it as though her life depended on it. Once there, her hand was trembling as she lifted the receiver. Maybe—oh, maybe it would be Rick!

It was Angela. She asked Lisa if she'd decided whether or not she was going to try out for cheerleader. Lisa swallowed hard and tried to keep her voice light as she said, "I don't think so. I'll be working on Saturdays and I hope after school."

"Then maybe I'll try out," Angela said. She laughed and added, "They'll only take three juniors, and I figured Sally and Evelyn have two of the spots sewed up. If you were trying out for the third, I wouldn't even bother."

"You have a good chance, I think," Lisa said. She didn't tell Angela that she wondered if either of them really would have had much of a chance. She suspected that she was too tall and Angela—well, Angela wasn't that special-looking. But you never know, and Lisa didn't want to make her newly recovered friend angry again.

"Guess Rick was pretty surprised about Patty, huh?" Angela said. "Is he terribly upset?"

Lisa felt fear strike her. So that was what this call was really about. Angela wasn't worried about the cheerleading thing at all. She had something to say about Rick and Patty. Lisa wanted to hang up before Angela could say anything else. She was afraid that Angela's gossip would destroy her hard-won strength, but she couldn't think of anything to say except, "I don't know what you're talking about."

"When Rick heard that Patty was engaged to that cowboy he must have really been upset. I mean, it's hard to imagine Patty living on a dude ranch, but it's also hard to imagine anyone dropping Rick Brewster."

"Patty's engaged?" Lisa asked. Her heart was beating so loudly she was sure that Angela would hear it over the telephone. But it was a beat of hope. If Patty was engaged to a cowboy on a dude ranch, then Rick would be free. Maybe he would come back to her!

Immediately, Lisa felt sorry for her selfish thoughts. As Angela went on, telling her that Patty couldn't stop talking about her wonderful summer, Lisa began to worry about Rick. Poor Rick. If Patty was really through with him, then he must feel just awful. She knew what a broken heart could feel like. She was sorry that Rick was finding out.

"They say Rick was really upset," Angela said. Her voice sounded almost happy.

"Look, I'll call you later," Lisa said.

"But you didn't tell me anything about Rick," Angela protested.

"No, I didn't," Lisa said and hung up. Too bad that she and Angela weren't friends after all, but it was clear from that conversation that they were not.

Lisa left a note for her mother saying she'd gone out for a walk. As she walked she tried to think of things to say to Rick that would make him feel better. She thought of telling him how much she admired him, of telling him he'd be better off without Patty, but everything seemed too silly to say. Somehow, she would have to find the words to console him. She would tell him that she understood his heartbreak and felt sorry for him. She would offer comfort without demands. She would begin by telling him that she was his friend, she decided.

Molly was really surprised to see her. She said, "Thought you were home sick?"

"I feel better now," Lisa said. "Rick here?"

"He's in the greenhouse watering plants," Molly said. Then she grinned. "I bet you two had another fight. True love never runs smooth or something."

"Something," Lisa agreed. "I want to talk to him. Is he real upset?"

"Not very," Molly answered. "I didn't even know you'd had a fight."

"We haven't," Lisa said. "It's about Patty."

"Oh, Patty," Molly said. "You don't have to worry about her."

"I'm not worried about Patty, I'm worried about Rick," Lisa grumbled as she went toward the greenhouse.

Rick was at the far end of the greenhouse, watering plants. He was wearing a baseball cap pulled back off his forehead and was whistling a tune as he worked. Lisa's first reaction was that he was being very brave. Then she looked at him more carefully and decided he was truly not very upset. Either Angela had the story wrong or Patty had already changed her mind. Whatever it was, Lisa had to know.

She began, "Rick, I just want us to be friends . . ."

Rick jumped and she realized he hadn't seen her come in. He said, "Hi, Lisa. I thought you were sick. I was coming over to your house later."

"No, I'm not sick," Lisa said. Then, because she didn't want to add to Rick's bad feelings, she said, "I wasn't feeling well this morning. But I'm better now."

"That's good," he said. Then he leaned over and kissed her quickly on the cheek. "Missed you."

"You don't have to pretend," Lisa said. "It's good you're being brave, if that's what you're being, but you don't have to pretend with me. I just want us to be friends."

Rick stopped, stared at her and said, "We are friends, Lisa. We've always been friends."

"But I want us to be real friends. I want you to understand that I understand."

"I want you to understand that I understand that you don't understand what you think you understand," Rick teased. "Or at least, I think I understand what you think you understand. Understand?"

"Rick, this is no time for jokes. I'm trying to be serious," Lisa said.

Rick laughed then and put down the hose. He put both arms around Lisa and pulled her close to him. "You heard some awful story about Patty breaking my heart, didn't you?"

"Yes."

"It's not true. No one could break my heart but you. You're the only heartbreaker I know. Now, are you going to start that stuff about friendship and understanding again, or are you going to be my girl?"

"I heard that Patty is in love . . . that she's engaged."

"Yes," Rick said. "I know that's what you heard. And I don't want anyone to hear anything different— except you. Can you keep a secret, Lisa?"

"Of course I can," Lisa answered. "But everyone knows about Patty's romance."

"This is the secret," he said as he leaned over and kissed her on the neck. "Patty didn't have a romance until I convinced her we were finished." Rick continued, "You didn't need to know this, but I was getting fed up with Patty a long time before she left for Colorado. Right after I'd dated you that first night, I wrote and told her it was all off. But she wouldn't believe me. There was no way to convince her until she came back and we could talk in person." He made a face. "Even then, it wasn't easy to convince her."

For one moment, Lisa wondered if Rick could be making all this up. Then she decided he would never do anything like that. He was too much of a gentleman ever to make up stories about a girl he'd been dating.

"I wish you'd told me," Lisa said.

"My father raised me to be a gentleman," Rick answered. "Even now, I feel guilty about talking to you about Patty. After all, Patty and I went together for a long time."

"So Patty made up the story to keep kids from feeling sorry for her?" Lisa asked.

"I guess that was the reason. She asked me not to tell anyone anything different. I promised." He looked at Lisa, waiting for her promise.

She smiled and put her arms around his neck. "Your secret is safe with me. But I'm glad your heart isn't broken. I hated that thought."

"My heart's never been in better shape," he assured her as they kissed.

Later, as they walked out of the shop and got into Rick's panel truck, Lisa asked, "Why didn't you call me for two days?"

"Were you worried?" Rick asked. "I told you I had to talk to her. Patty doesn't convince easily."

Rick pulled away from the curb and they started riding toward the lake. Soon they were on the main highway, whizzing by farmland and open scenery. Lisa trailed her hand out the window, letting the cool air play through her fingers. She said, "I still can't believe the way things worked out. I worried all summer about what was going to happen when Patty came back to town."

Rick glanced at her with surprise. "You weren't really worried?"

"Yes," Lisa said softly. "I was worried. And you never said anything about Patty at all. Why didn't you tell me what you were thinking?"

"Why didn't you ask if you were worried? You never said a word about Patty. I thought you knew it was finished."

"I didn't dare ask," Lisa admitted. "But it seemed to me that you must still be thinking of her—or else you would have said something. You can't imagine what I imagined," she added.

"I told you I am a gentleman," Rick said lightly.

Lisa knew he was giving her a serious answer even if his voice was light. Rick really was a gentleman in many ways. He was always courteous to people, never asked nosy questions and always took responsibility for his actions. She supposed he thought it was wrong to talk about old girlfriends.

"You're nice," Lisa said. "I guess I didn't give you enough credit for being the person you are. And I guess I didn't give myself enough credit either. I have a hard time believing you really care about me."

"I care," Rick said. "I care a lot. But I want you to promise me that next time you are worried about something—anything at all—you'll ask me about it. Will you promise?"

"Yes, I promise," Lisa said.

They pulled into the lake parking lot. Lisa sighed and said, "It's over. Summer is over and school begins tomorrow. I hate to see it go."

Rick put his arm around her shoulder and hugged her close to him. He said, "There will be other summers."

"Yes," Lisa agreed. As she sat beside Rick, looking out at the lake she realized that she truly believed there would be other wonderful summers for them. The fear of the future was gone. Even so, she said, "But nothing will ever be any better than this summer. This was special. I'll always think of it as my summer of flowers."

"Lisa, beautiful Lisa," Rick murmured as he turned her toward him. "You will always be surrounded by flowers and love."

If you enjoyed this book...

...you will enjoy a *First Love* from Silhouette subscription even more. It will bring you each new title, as soon as it is published every month, delivered right to your door.

Filled with the challenges, excitement and anticipation that make first love oh, so wonderful, *First Love* romances are new and different. Every *First Love* romance is an original novel—never before published—and all written by leading authors.

If you enjoyed this book, treat yourself, or some friend, to a one-year subscription to these romantic originals. We'll ship two NEW $1.75 romances each month, a total of 24 books a year. So send in your coupon now. **There's nothing quite as special as a First Love.**

First Love from Silhouette

NEW BOY IN TOWN
Sixteen-year-old Stacey Hippner loves her parents but she resents their restrictions—especially when they involve Garr Garwin, the new boy in town.

KATE HERSELF
Kate Fleming had always felt the insignificant middle sister. That was before Ross Barrow, the most popular boy in school asked her out.

PLEASE LET ME IN
Melissa Johnson had always dreamed of being in with the most popular crowd. When Greg Scott, hero of the high school football team, begins to date her, she feels she has really made it.

FLOWERS FOR LISA
Lisa Kelly's interest in flowers earns her a summer job at Rick Brewster's father's florist shop. She is thrilled when she and Rick start dating. But she wonders if their relationship will turn out to be only a summer romance.

GIRL IN THE ROUGH
Kate's life as the brainy big sister of adorable, popular Mimi was not easy. When Kate took up golf all this changed.

First Love from Silhouette

THERE'S NOTHING
QUITE AS SPECIAL AS A
<u>FIRST LOVE</u>.

_____#1 **NEW BOY IN TOWN**   **$1.75**
         Dorothy Francis

_____#2 **GIRL IN THE ROUGH**   **$1.75**
         Josephine Wunsch

_____#3 **PLEASE LET ME IN**   **$1.75**
         Patti Beckman

_____#4 **SERENADE**   **$1.75**
         Adrienne Marceau

_____#5 **FLOWERS FOR LISA**   **$1.75**
         Veronica Ladd

_____#6 **KATE HERSELF**   **$1.75**
         Helen Erskine

FIRST LOVE, Department FL/3
1230 Avenue of the Americas
New York, NY 10020

Please send me the books I have checked above. I am enclosing $_____ (please add 50¢
to cover postage and handling. NYS and NYC residents please add appropriate sales tax).
Send check or money order—no cash or C.O.D.'s please. Allow six weeks for delivery.

NAME_____

ADDRESS_____

CITY_____STATE/ZIP_____